# APACHE
## The Long Ride Home

*Grant Gall*

## REAL WEST
### FICTION SERIES

*Sunstone Press • Santa Fe • New Mexico*

*For my lovely wife, POH-TUAN,*
*Whose Oriental gentleness*
*Is my strength.*

All of the characters in this book
are fictitious, and any resemblance
to actual persons, living or dead,
is purely coincidental.

First Edition

Printed in the United States of America

---

Library of Congress Cataloging in Publication Data:

Gall, Grant, 1935-
  Apache: the long ride home.

  1. Apache Indians--Fiction. I. Title.
PS3557.A41152.A63    1987    813'.54    87-10137
ISBN: 0-86534-105-2

---

Published in 1988 by SUNSTONE PRESS
            Post Office Box 2321
            Santa Fe, NM 87504-2321 / USA

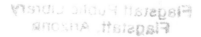

# ACKNOWLEDGEMENTS

For a variety of reasons I am indebted to many people. The list which follows is of those to whom I owe the most.

The late Paul I. Wellman, author and historian par excellence, of Los Angeles, California, who provided me with the initial impetus. Dan L. Thrapp, of Whittier, California, in my opinion the greatest living authority concerning the Apache wars, who prevented me taking a wrong trail, Professor C.L. Sonnichsen, of El Paso, Texas, and the late Colonel Wilbur S. Nye, of Wormleysburg, Pennsylvania, author-historians both, who each provided me with excellent leads. Mr. K.J. Lace, County Librarian, and his staff at the Essex County Library, The Chief Librarian, Ministry of Defence Library (Central and Army), London, and his staff. These last two were invaluable sources of difficult to obtain reference works. Gene B. Kuntz, of Santa Fe, New Mexico, for his much valued assistance. And Miss Irene Lawson who did the lion's share of the typing. But the last shall be first and my greatest debt is to John A. (Bud) Shapard, of the Bureau of Indian Affairs, Washington, who read the manuscript and made a number of most welcome comments and suggestions. Bud's lovely wife, Juanita, is a great-granddaughter of the famous Apache chief, Loco.

"No Indian has more virtues
and none has been more truly
ferocious when aroused."

*Captain John Bourke, adjutant to
Indian fighter General George Crook,
concerning the Apaches.*

# PREFACE

This novel is an obituary. It is an obituary to a way of life which ended when the final vestiges of Apache Indian resistance crumbled before the might of the United States after a relentless fifty year struggle for possession of the vast American Southwest.

The clash between red and white was inevitable. Yet to say that its origins lie in disputes concerning territorial ownership would be entirely superficial. It was much more than that. It was the head-on collision of two ways of life which were totally incompatible. Where there could be no possible understanding until the conflict had ended in the absolute subjugation of one by the other.

No attempt has been made to judge either side. But instead to recreate from an Indian viewpoint a vanished aspect of America's colourful and bloody heritage.

Only the characters and episodes interwoven into the overall fabric of that epic struggle are the creations of my imagination. Everything else is as it was, without leading the reader into the quagmire of minute and boring detail.

Both the Apache way of life and its final total eclipse by the remorseless westward onslaught of the United States are seen through the eyes of a retired sheepherder who lived through all that occurred during those last despairing years. This story belongs to him so let the telling of it be his.

# CHAPTER ONE

It is too hot out here. You do not think so? When you are as old as I am you will think so. Come inside. It is cooler and there are fewer flies to bother us. Ah, this is much better. Sit down please. Maria, fetch the young man a beer.

You must forgive me senor if I seem to stare at you. But you say you are a reporter for a New York magazine and this puzzles me. What can you want with us that you have come so far? Nothing ever happens out here. Gracias, Maria. You are surprised senor that beer so cold can be found in a village that is without gas or electricity. But, like many of our friends, we have an ice house and a truck calls once a week with fresh ice. It is the most important event of the week. So what can you want with a little Mexican village where the biggest occasion on the calendar is the arrival of an ice truck?

It is not the village you came to see? You came to see me? You want to talk about my life? You joke, senor. I am nobody. Just a retired sheepherder who likes to sit outside when it is not too hot. And to sit inside when it is. In the evenings I like to visit the cantina and talk with my friends over a glass or two of tequilla. Your readers would soon become bored with such a story.

Apache? Me? You are mistaken. It is as I have told you. I am just a retired Mexican sheepherder. What was I before that? Obviously, senor, a sheepherder. You think this was not so? You are wrong. I do not lie. How long was I a sheepherder? I can see that you are a persistent young man. Your eye is like that of the hawk before it swoops. You sense a story just as the hawk senses its prey.

You are right of course. There has been much more to my life than sheepherding. You have had strong information or you would not be here. It could be, however, that I will not add to that information. But you have come a great distance. I do not like to disappoint such determination. It is a good thing in one so young.

Besides, the truth cannot hurt me now. I am too old. The wars between the Indians and the Americans are no more. The old ways are ended forever. And no one is interested in punishing a harmless old man like me. Yes senor, I was once an Apache warrior. I rode with Coletto Negro on his great raid into the United States. But I was born a Mexican.

My parents were of peon stock. They were poor, persecuted and always afraid. Afraid of their masters, afraid of bandits, afraid of the Apaches . . . What is that senor? A tape recorder. Yes, of course. I have seen such things in mail order catalogues. Much easier than writing. And more accurate? That is good. But how can it work without electricity? From batteries? Of course. Please forgive an old man's stupidity . . . afraid that the crops might fail and they would go hungry, afraid that there might be a good harvest and the taxes would be high or the bandits or Apaches would come.

The Apaches adopted me when I was nine years old. The processes of become an orphan and my subsequent adoption were short and sharp. Short in time. Sharp in violence. I can remember it as though it were but yesterday that it happened.

# CHAPTER TWO

From its perch high in the blue sky the sun relentlessly poured its golden heat down upon our village. A solitary white wisp of cloud hung motionless as if time and gravity were non-existent. That cloud was much like our village. Life there had changed very little for perhaps two or three hundred years. People were born, grew up, married, had their children and died without ever leaving the village.

On this day I was walking across the plaza with my father and mother . . . You know, senor, after more than eighty years I find it impossible to recall either of them with emotion . . . We were setting out to visit some relatives, of my mother I believe, in another village about five miles away. We walked because we were too poor to own even one horse.

Before we reached the other side of the plaze where commenced the road which linked the two villages, the Apaches were upon us. It was soon finished. There was the sudden sound of unshod Indian ponies, a glimpse of almost naked brown bodies, the heavy odour of sweating horses and cries of war mixed with screams of terror.

When all was quiet and still again my life had been changed forever. Both my mother and father were dead. My father, in trying to protect my mother, had been cut almost to pieces. I stared down at them both. Their blood stained my feet. Yet I could not cry.

An Apache warrior bent down from his horse, its glossy black flanks still heaving from exertion, to pick me up. As his hand grabbed my arm I bit hard into the flesh of his forearm. It was a deep bite and he shouted with pain. The other Apaches laughed loudly at his discomfort.

He reached down again. I tried the same tactic but this time he was too quick. He jerked me upwards onto his horse and sat me in front of him. I fought like a cornered bobcat, spitting, biting and clawing. He struck me on the back of the neck. A vivid flash, then darkness.

# CHAPTER THREE

When I became conscious again, I was immediately aware of the gentle jogging movement of the horse beneath me. I was lying face down across its neck. The sun was hot through my cotton shirt and there was an ache in the back of my head.

For a while I did not move. Things came back to me slowly. Tears misted my eyes and dropped onto the dusty ground beneath the horse's belly. Crying was no good, I told myself. Apaches despised cowardice. I had heard my father say so.

The dust churned up by the horse's hooves found its way into my mouth and nostrils. I started coughing. An Apache riding alongside grunted something to the warrior seated behind me.

My captor placed his hand on my back and spoke to me in almost perfect Spanish. "Buenas dias little wild one. How is your head?"

His voice was mocking but not without, I felt, a faint hint of respect for my fighting spirit. As he spoke his arm circled my waist, lifted me and placed me firmly astride the horse's neck. I looked straight ahead, determined to show no fear.

The warrior riding beside us spoke again but in the gutteral Apache tongue which I did not then understand. My captor translated for me. "He says that you will grow into a fine fighting man one day." He laughed. "And then you too will fight Mexicans."

I bit deeply into my lower lip to prevent myself from crying. Tears clouded my eyes but I kept looking at the horse's head so that neither the Apache behind me nor the one beside me could see them. Yes, I would become a warrior as soon as I was old enough. But it would not be Mexicans that I killed. It would be Apaches. I would kill until there were none left.

There was no more talk for a time. As we rode in silence I recalled my father once telling me that it was a common practice among the Apache people to abduct young boys from other Indian tribes and Mexican villages in order to bring them up as their own. He had even heard of white "Apaches" and black "Apaches." These were the children of the gringos and Negroes who lived north of the border.

The hot desert air soon dried my eyes so I no longer had any need to hide them. I glanced sideways at the warrior who had spoken first. He was typical of his race. About five and a half feet tall and muscular with a copper-coloured skin. His somewhat broad head was set on a squat, thickset neck. The face was well-formed with high cheekbones and eyes as black as the night sky when there is no moon. His mouth was neither mean nor generous. Like all Apaches, men and women, his thick black hair grew long. It was kept from his eyes by a band of bright red cloth tied around his head above the ears. He had neither beard nor moustache. I learned later that such sparse hairs as did appear on their faces were soon removed with the aid of home-made tweezers. He was clad only in a muslin breech clout and long moccasins. The latter had been turned down to a point just below the knee.

This same warrior spoke to my captor again, who in turn, addressed me in Spanish as before: "Lobo says that if we are to make an Apache of you then you must learn to speak our language. So, little one . . ."

"My name is not little one," I interrupted fiercely. "It is Pedro Bautista."

"So you have a tongue. We were beginning to think you were a mute. But . . ." he laughed mockingly. ". . . Pedro is no name for a young Apache warrior. It is not strong enough. It is not a name at all. What shall we call you?"

Lobo spoke. But, although in the Apache tongue, I detected one word of Spanish — 'cuchillo' which means 'knife'.

"Lobo says that your teeth cut into my arm like the blade of a knife. He thinks we should name you Cuchillo. So be it. From this time on you are called Cuchillo."

I wanted to protest that this was not my name. That it was Pedro. Pedro Bautista. But, inside, I already knew that such protests would be as a battering ram of feathers against a thick adobe wall. So the words formed in my mind died before they reached my throat. Anyway, I consoled myself, Cuchillo was a Spanish name.

It is a strange fact that the Apaches so often adopted the Spanish names give to them by the Mexicans in preference to those conferred in their own language. This was the case with many of their great leaders including Mangas Coloradas (Red Sleeves) and Victorio (Victorious).

As we rode, the warrior seated behind me pointed in turn at the many things around us. He would give each object two names. The first in Spanish. The second in Apache. This second name he would make me repeat until I did so without a mistake. So, gradually and reluctantly, I learned the Apache words for mountain, river, canyon, rattlesnake, desert, sky, sun, cactus and so many others that my head felt it would soon burst.

# CHAPTER FOUR

At noon the war party, I counted twenty-five in it, halted at the edge of a cool running spring concealed on all sides by tall outcrops of red rock that seemed to grow straight out of the desert floor. It had been a long ride, dry and hot. My captor dismounted from behind me and lifted me from his horse. The other Apaches **were already watering their mounts and packhorses and enjoying the coolness of the spring.**

For the first time since we had started on the ride I was able to see my Indian foster father. He was above average height for an Apache and lean. I was shocked. He did not have a cruel face. Warmth and humour were in his eyes.

He pointed to the waters of the spring that danced and sparkled in the sun. "Drink."

My pride told me not to. But thirst in a young boy is an easy victor over pride. Like the Apaches already at the water I lay on my stomach and drank. It was good.

After a while I sat back, refreshed but hungry. The lean one, the others called him Coletto Negro, which means Black Tail, thrust some dried meat into my hands. I did not know what animal it came from and cared not. I just ate. It was tough but not without flavour.

My hunger appeased, I looked around hopefully. But there were no other captives. Never had I felt so lonely. Several of the warriors were standing waist-deep in the water, splashing each other like children in a fountain. It was difficult to imagine that but a few hours earlier these same men had ruthlessly murdered helpless men and women.

But that is how it was with the Apache. He lived by war and the plunder it brought him. War was not a sport as it was with the Indians of the plains further north. It was his life. Or death. The desert was his home but it grew no crops. Neither was it possible to rear livestock there. Mexicans were his sheep and he sheared them regularly.

Although the Apache lived by raiding it was not his way to be unnecessarily daring in battle. His was the way of the guerilla, the sniper, the ambusher. Hit and run tactics were his trade mark. It was not that he lacked courage but that he regarded life as his most valuable possession and sold it dearly. To an Apache the chivalry displayed by the plains Indians in their battles was little short of insanity. Accordingly, he left the heroics to them and carried on with his lifelong business of living.

After a period of horseplay most of the warriors squatted on their heels in the shadows of the rocks and chewed at strips of dried meat. The remaining few sought vantage points so that they could watch all directions for possible pursuit by the Mexican regulars. All this was done without orders of any kind being given.

At first I had considered the possibility of my rescue by the Mexican militia, but had soon dismissed it from my thoughts. Our soldiers were mainly convicts conscripted from local prisons and they had no stomachs for fighting. If they pursued us at all it would be at a safe distance. Then they would return to camp with the usual report of fictitious skirmishes with the raiding party during which one or two Apaches were killed, several wounded and the remainder escaped with their injured and dead.

Not that the troops had any need to worry about catching up with the marauders. An Apache war party was as elusive as the shadow of an eagle in flight. No, their main concern was that the Apaches did not turn about and catch up with them.

The respite in the shade of the rocks was brief. The pack-animals carrying the plunder from our village were brought into line by the remounted warriors and the cavalcade continued its way northward beneath the merciless sun.

To the Apaches such heat was merely part of the long, unvaried pattern of life. But not my life. At this time of the day all Mexicans were happily engaged in the traditional siesta. With the exception of myself of course. Wherever I looked there was the sun like a disc of white hot iron direct from the forge. The heat made my head feel lighter and, after a short time, my eyes started to distort the images of things around me. Unconsciousness began to invade my mind.

Seated behind me Coletto Negro could not see my face but he must have been aware of my condition. He guided his mount across to one of the packhorses, took a Mexican straw hat from a bundle on its back and placed it squarely on my head. His voice was gentle and for my ears alone. "You are brave like an Apache boy. You do not complain. That is good." Despite a desire not to feel proud, I grew several inches taller at these words and sat straighter.

As my eyes slowly recovered from the sun's onslaught and the hat's wide brim protected them from further attack, I began to look around me. Grandeur and colour were everywhere. There was grandeur in the rugged structure and immensity of the desert. Colour in its massive rocky barriers, sparse shrubs and the tenacious, ever-present cactus.

We did not stop again until the sun turned from white hot to fiery red and plunged behind the distant mountains in a blaze of unbelievable colour. As the shadows of the dying day lengthened into darkness the Apaches slowly guided their weary mounts and packhorses into a small natural fortress of virtually impregnable rocks.

This was their pattern, to travel by day and to rest by night. But I was not aware of it that night. I was asleep before Coletto Negro lifted me from his horse.

# CHAPTER FIVE

After three days and nights we arrived on the heights above a small copper-mining village in southern New Mexico. Overlooking the Mexican-owned mines was the camp of Pablo Azul, chief of a small band of Chiricahua Apaches. As we approached the camp the warriors stiffened visibly in their saddles. They now rode erect with eyes looking straight ahead and faces expressionless.

As we entered the outskirts of the Apache village we were immediately surrounded by laughing children and a multicoloured pack of flea-ridden mongrel curs which yapped and snapped at the horses' heels. Still the warriors looked straight ahead. Still with expressionless faces. From the centre of the camp could be heard the chant: "They are coming. They are coming."

The triumphant war party herded all the packhorses into a milling circle in a large open space, which must have been the equivalent of our village plaza, and solemnly dismounted from their ponies. Coletto Negro lifted me from his mount and handed me the reins. "Hold him. I will be back."

He strode across to where the other warriors, weary and streaked with dust and vermillion, were already unloading the pack-animals. It had been a good raid. For the Apaches that is. There was much plunder and not a man had been lost or even injured. Unless you count the bite I gave Coletto Negro.

The Apache way of life was that of a supremely democratic community. When the spoils were divided the rest of the community took precedence over the warriors. The chief, who was such only as long as his people desired it, came last of all. He was the most capable mentally and physically, or he would not be chief, so he required least from the communal pool.

First came the elderly and the seriously disabled, then came the widows and divorcees followed by the warriors and their families. Their leader, Pablo Azul, was not there however. Instead, he was examining me closely from a distance of two or three feet. An ugly man, his stomach and face were bloated by excessive drinking and eating.

He spoke rapidly in perfect Spanish: "Why are you here? Who brought you?"

Fear caused a dryness in my mouth and the answer would not come. He took a pace closer and raised a hand as if to strike me. "Are you deaf, boy?" he grated from between clenched teeth. "Who brought you here?"

A second fear overcame the first and I stammered: "Coletto

13

Negro.''

The chief turned around and waddled over to the warrior I had named. He spoke to him and pointed in my direction. Soon a fierce argument developed between them. It was in their own tongue so I would not have understood even if I had been able to hear them distinctly. Their words rapidly became even more heated and several other members of the raiding party joined in. They seemed to be siding with Coletto Negro. Suddenly, Pablo Azul thrust his arms outward in angry resignation and strode off as fast as his fat legs would allow.

Many years later I learned the cause of the quarrel. For a number of years the wily and greedy old Chiricahua chief had been dipping both hands into separate honey pots. One hand offered friendship to the Mexican mine-owners for the gifts, particularly whisky, that his protection brought in return. The other hand directed the traditional raids deep into Sonora and Chihuahua for the spoils they brought.

But the raids differed from those of the old days in two ways. The first was that the chief no longer led them himself. The second was that they were solely for plunder. The taking of captives was forbidden. The reason for both changes was the same. It was to keep his Mexican neighbours at the copper mines ignorant of his continued criminal campaigns against their fellow countrymen to the south.

Truly remarkable were the strength of the chief's personality and the depth of his cunning. The marauding continued, the miners remained ignorant of it, his corpulence increased and his authority was seldom questioned.

But Coletto Negro had seen something in me that had made him want to rear me as his own son. Accordingly, he had brought me back with him. And Pablo Azul, feeling that his leadership was being threatened, had made an issue of it, only to withdraw before overwhelming odds when Coletto Negro, supported by the others, had sworn never to let me approach the Mexican miners. It was a promise they kept religiously.

The division of the spoils continued. Each took only what he or she needed and no more. Some took clothing, others took blankets or household utensils. Everyone took corn. There was no livestock. Our village was agricultural and the few animals the villages did possess were all hide and bone and kept only for their milk. What little meat clung to their skinny frames would soon have disappeared during the long, arid, grassless trek northward.

That night a dance was held to celebrate the success of the

raid. I saw nothing of it, however, for I was confined to Coletto Negro's wickiup, a dome-shaped structure of curved saplings covered with brush. All young children were kept inside their parents' homes on such occasions. But I could not sleep. The monotonous rhythmic drumming that accompanied the dancing made me strangely exicted. For two or three hours I could not close my ears to it or to the chanting of the warriors as they relived their attack on my village. All this time I moved restlessly on the animal skin beneath me which was my bed. But it had been a long, eventful day and sleep is too powerful an opponent for a weary nine-year-old boy to combat indefinitely. Inevitably, I lost and sleep invaded my mind completely.

# CHAPTER SIX

The following morning I was jolted back to consciousness by someone jerking the animal skin from under me. I rolled over on the hard earth floor of the wickiup and immediately fell asleep again. A hand grabbed my shoulder and shook it roughly. It was Coletto Negro. "Wake up!" he thundered in mock anger. "Your snoring has scared the moon away and the sun has taken its place in the sky. It is time to commence your training as a warrior."

I pulled away from him and dropped to the floor again. "I do not want to be a warrior," I protested. "I want to sleep."

"You have slept enough." He picked me up, thrust me under his right arm and carried me struggling from the wickiup. The sun's brightness struck me in the eyes like a blow from a fist. For a brief moment the shock caused me to stop fighting. But my arms and legs were soon thrashing the air again.

Somewhere behind us I could hear Lobo laughing. "Watch for his teeth," he called. However, I was in no position to bite Coletto Negro. He had seen to that.

He did not break his stride until we reached a swift-running stream a short distance from the camp. Without warning he dropped me into its icy waters. I rose quickly to the surface, kicking and spluttering. There was a panic inside me. I could not breathe without taking in water. He was trying to kill me. Then, suddenly, my feet touched the stream bed. When I straightened my body the water barely reached my shoulders. I looked sheepishly at the man who had thrown me in.

But tears of laughter prevented him seeing me. His entire body was shaking with mirth. He tried to say something but laughter changed the words to a gurgle in his throat. After a few seconds he was able to speak. "What kind of fighting man is this?" he asked. "He attacks an entire stream single-handed. Without any . . ." Suddenly, laughter had him firmly in its grip again.

By now, the initial shock of being thrown into water chilled by the night frosts had left me. I could not swim but the stream was not deep and I was soon enjoying the freshness of the water. It was quite exhilarating. For some reason I cannot recall, perhaps it was relief that he had not been trying to drown me, I started splashing Coletto Negro as he stood laughing beside the stream.

He leaped backwards but slipped on some loose pebbles and found himself sitting in a small, muddy pool. He was still laughing, however, and, enjoying the humour of his situation, I continued to splash him. Suddenly, recalling my dead father and mother, I stopped. The bitterness had returned to my heart and the smile disappeared from my face. Coletto Negro must have known my thoughts although he did not say so. But he stopped laughing, reached out an arm and jerked me from the stream.

"Now we must dry you," he said, pointing to a pillar of red rock about a half-mile distant. "Run to that rock as fleetly as your legs will carry you and return to me. Do not stop or run too slowly. **For if you do either then I will beat you with this stick."** He **thwacked a mean-looking rod of willow against the palm of his** other hand. I could almost feel it across my buttocks.

I started running. I would show him that a Mexican boy was as good as any Apache boy. Soon my heart was pounding like the drums of the previous night. My mouth was dry and my empty stomach felt as if it was being torn apart. The sun was a bright golden cymbal in the cloudless sky but, as it was still early morning, it was low enough on the horizon not to be too hot.

At the rock I turned without stopping and started back. My legs were like so much uncontrollable rubber, my eyes were clouded with tears and sweat, my windpipe felt as raw as an open wound but I would not give in. Without warning hand came through the red haze that floated before my eyes and stopped me in mid-stride. This abrupt halt to the pressure on my heart was too much and I fainted.

As I slowly recovered consciousness I could hear Coletto Negro chuckling. "You have much spirit. You would have kept running until the mountains stopped you. This is good. A fighting man needs such qualities."

# CHAPTER SEVEN

So began my initiation into the apprenticeship which every Apache boy had to undertake before he could become a warrior. It was a gruelling test of all the qualities that made a real man. And each day was tougher than the one it followed. Several boys underwent their training at the same time and, before long, I was thrust into competition against a dozen or more of my own age. We wrestled, threw small rocks, sometimes at each other, to quicken our reactions and to learn to withstand silently the pains of not being quick enough, competed with bow and arrow and raced on foot.

I do not boast when I say that I excelled in all these things. My prowess came from a burning desire not to be beaten in any event by the Apache boys. Inevitably, I did lose on occasions but these were rare. It is fortunate that they were for whenever I lost I would go to a quiet place and bite my arms in silent fury and frustration. At such times Coletto Negro would notice the marks in my flesh but he never once questioned me about them. I am certain he knew how they came there.

That he was proud of me I was well aware. The Apaches were inveterate gamblers. They would wager everything on anything. And Coletto Negro would back me against the other boys whenever the opportunity arose, which was often. At first I was torn between deliberately losing, as a means of punishing him for taking me from my people, and a selfish desire not to be beaten. But my pride was ever victorious and the prestige that winning brought gave me an intense feeling of satisfaction. Soon I became over-confident.

Complacency is a poor companion. One day I was matched against an older Apache boy whose parents had recently joined our band. He was tall, sinewy and fairer skinned than the rest of us. It was a foot-race over a distance of about six miles. Coletto Negro had added as a sidestake to his original bet of a Mexican saddle his beautiful black war-pony. There were only two of us in the race which was held early in the morning. The entire village was there to watch.

The starting signal was to be a yellow bandana dropped to the ground by Lobo who, like many others, had backed me heavily. I glanced at the other boy as he crouched beside me awaiting the signal. He did not appear nervous. He must have sensed I was looking at him because his face turned towards me briefly. In that second or two I saw only one thing, his blue eyes. Never before had I seen an Apache with blue eyes. It was . . .

The yellow bandana left Lobo's outstretched hand and floated lazily downwards. Everything other than the long race ahead was immediately swept from my mind. I was quickly into my stride, long and rhythmic. Encouarged by the many voices screaming at me to win, I soon left my fair-skinned competitor trailing. Confidence surged through every muscle as the distance between us slowly increased. The sound of his footsteps retreated gradually until I could hear them no more. After a mile or so I looked back. He was three or four hundred yards behind. I looked ahead again and felt good.

Many minutes later I glanced back a second time and saw that the distance between us remained unchanged. The line of the race was roughly circular, and would end where it had started. My breathing was still even and controlled. There was much power left in my legs. I would show them. I would run the skinny one into the earth. He would not even be in sight when I finished. Sucking the hot, dry air deeper into my lungs I almost sprinted the next half mile.

With my chest sitll heaving from the increased exertion, I eased the pace sufficiently to look for the runner behind me. My eyes were lying, I told myself. The slender one was closer than before. His running was ungainly, yet he did not appear to be labouring. Mastering the panic that has seized my stomach in its icy claws, I ran as if life itself was the prize.

The familiar landmarks that surrounded the camp could now be seen ahead. The pace was beginning to affect me, however. I felt as if a hundred knives were stabbing into my chest, my legs were heavy like so much rock and there was the taste of blood in my mouth. As I ran it now seemed that I was motionless, and that the village was moving slowly towards me through a mist. I could hear people shouting and screaming. My body tried to respond to this encouragement but could not. Then I heard the sound of running feet crunching into the sand behind me; and knew I had lost.

# CHAPTER EIGHT

I can recall nothing more until I opened my eyes and saw the roof of the wickiup above me. My body felt as if I had been buried alive by a rock fall. Although every movement caused me pain, I sat up slowly and looked around. I was alone. Coletto Negro must have carried me there and then left me to recover. He had no wife. She had died a year ago giving birth to the son he had always wanted. But the baby had lived only a few days. He had not remarried. At that moment I was grateful for the solitude. For some time I sat there just thinking. I blinked back tears brought by the memory of defeat. It was too much for me. I had to go to my quiet place among the rocks and trees that skirted the river. I stood up. The torture of doing so caused sweat to pour from my aching body.

The sun was still high in the sky as I emerged from the low opening of the brush shelter. How long I had been unconscious I did not know — but it could not have been more than an hour or so, for the men of the village were still preparing for a deer hunt into the distant mountains. Such preparations were made in the morning. The hunt would take most of the day, and the men would return late in the evening. If their luck was good there would be much feasting that night.

Practically everyone was engaged in the business that always preceded the hunt, and no one saw me leave the village. Once beyond the outer circle of dwellings that formed the village boundary, I turned and looked back. The men were now mounting their hunting ponies; sturdy, fast, sure-footed animals. Many of the older boys were also there. For some it would be their first hunt. I envied them. Already, I was beginning to forget my Mexican heritage and yearn for the thrills and glory of Apache manhood. But the transition taking place within me was gradual and I did not then recognize or even suspect it. To me the feelings I experienced were the natural yearnings of a young boy. The hunters galloped from the other side of the camp, raising dust which slowly subsided as they faded from sight. I continued walking. As the sun's heat seeped through my skin the soreness slowly disappeared from my body until but one ache remained. And that was in my heart.

Seated on a rock, warmed by those slanting shafts of sunlight which suceeded in piercing the thick bushes concealing my quiet place, I reflected on the pain of losing. Now, to an old man well past his ninetieth year it appears in its correct perspective; a triviality, nothing more, in a life that has experienced so many other things of far greater importance. But at that time, to a ten-year-old boy who had just been humbled before his entire village and caused his foster parent to lose a magnificent war pony, it was the father and mother of all disasters. My mind thought of many things. I considered the possibility of running away and finding my way back to Mexico. But the desert was big and frightening and, like most children, I had a powerful imagination. Before long I was terrifying myself with mental pictures of rattlesnakes, scorpions, tarantulas, lizards, mountain lions and, the strongest argument of all against escape, pursuit by angry Apaches.

Any further conjecture was halted abruptly by the noisy movement of someone or something in the brush immediately in front of me. A moment of fear followed by apprehension. Silently, I slid into cover behind the rock on which I had been sitting. The sound of bushes being forced apart, and then swishing together again, stopped and and a light brown face with blue eyes was soon framed in the thicket a few feet ahead. My conqueror of a few hours earlier looked around cautiously and then stepped into the clearing. As I moved suddenly from concealment to confront him he started visibly, but quickly relaxed. I felt savagely pleased at his obvious embarrassment.

"I am called Cabeza," he said simply. "How are you called?"

Unbalanced by this friendly directness I answered in imperfect Apache, "They call me Cuchillo."

"You do not speak like an Apache," he commented bluntly.

"And you do not look like an Apache," I replied, equally curt.

"This is true." He hesitated briefly, then continued. "It is because I am not an Indian. But they do not like me to remember that I am not of their race. It angers them if I speak of it. But, inside, I feel that I can trust you and can talk to you without fear. I will tell you how it was." He sat on a rock and I squatted, Apache-style, on my heels. "My parents were American and . . ." He stopped. "You smile. Why is this?"

"I smile because I was born a Mexican. A Mexican who was cursing himself but a few minutes ago for permitting an Apache to outrun him. But the Apache is an American and I no longer feel so bad about being beaten." Now he too was grinning. Our smiles grew and soon we were both laughing. And with this laughter any remaining barriers between us crumbled.

Cabeza wiped the tears from his eyes with the back of his hand. "It is good to laugh again," he said. "It has been a long time since I spoke with one who was not Apache." He face was sombre again. "My father and mother were both born in Tennessee. They were born and raised there. But after they were married father could never settle in one place for long. And wherever he decided to go mother went without complaining. She was a strong yet gentle person and he loved her in his way. But his way was not easy. He was never able to overcome the urge to keep moving westward. If the Indians had not stopped him, I think he would have kept on until we all drowned in the great ocean beyond the snow-crested mountains.

"I was born in Missouri, but we moved on again when I was little more than one year old. The pattern repeated itself through Kansas; and into Texas where we owned a strip of good land, well-watered and fertile. But father had heard there was even better soil awaiting the plough in New Mexico. Friends tried to dissuade him. They told him that the land was dry and unsuited to farming. That the Apaches were raiding again after years of comparative peace. There would be no military protection, they said, because the soldiers were too busy fighting each other in the east. But he would not listen. He loaded the wagon, hitched the horses and cracked his whip high over their broad backs.

"A small band of mounted Apaches struck us fifteen or twenty miles east of Santa Fe. There was a running fight for a few hundred yards. Mother took the reins while father climbed into the rear of the wagon and started shooting over the tailgate at the screaming, paint-streaked warriors. He pushed me to the floor and told me to keep my head down. I had never been so afraid. My tears made small dark spots in the grey alkaline dust that coated the wagon bed. Despite my father's orders, I raised my head until I could see the Indians through a narrow slit in the canvas cover. One galloped his horse alongside and tried to pull mother from her seat. She lashed at him with the whip but lost control of the terrified horses. The wagon overturned. Mother was thrown high into the air and landed in a crumpled heap. She must have died instantly for she did not move again. One warrior dismounted and prodded her with his foot, but a bullet ploughed a bloody furrow across his back. He remounted hastily and rejoined the others who were warily circling father at a respectful distance.

"He just stood there, the wrecked wagon in pieces all round him, calmly shooting at the Apaches as they tired to close with him. I was trapped in the tangle of ripped canvas and splintered woodwork but he was too busy levering and firing his rifle to notice my predicament. A bullet from his repeater struck a warrior squarely in the chest. The others suddenly lost interest in taking him alive and just shot him down like a mad dog that had to be killed. I tried not to cry but I could not stop myself sobbing as he fell. They heard me and searched the wreckage. One of them dragged me into the open and jerked me to my feet. After poking and pinching my flesh, as a livestock judge would that of a prize boar, they put me on an already overloaded pack-mule and took me with them. The bodies of my parents were left to the weather and wild animals.''

"But what made your father keep moving on as he did?'' I asked Cabeza, remembering how my own father and many generations before him had never lived anywhere other than in the village which had been their home from birth to death.

"I never knew. I do not think that even he knew. It was not to find better land as he said. This was just an excuse. Not the reason. But whatever he was searching for he never found it. And how was it with you? Was your family also moving west?''

"No. It was different with us. Much different. Mexicans do not have to go anywhere to find the Apaches. They come looking for us. They have done so for hundreds of years. Whatever they want from us they take, even our lives, and we let them. For them, and for us I fear, it is an accepted way of life.''

"But why do the Mexicans accept it? Why do they not fight when the Apaches attack?''

Suddenly I felt ashamed of my people; for the first time in my life I despised their weakness. "Because we are cowards!'' I blurted out angrily. "We are born afraid and we die afraid. It has ever been so.''

"But you are not a coward.'' Cabeza's voice was gentle but his words were strong. "When you raced against me this morning you would have run yourself to death rather than surrender. I could see it when I turned to watch you finish.''

"Then I did finish? I can remember nothing after you passed me.''

"That is why I say you are not a coward. You were unconscious on your feet, but your fighting spirit carried you the rest of the way. You did not collapse until you reached Lobo. All who saw it were impressed. There were many words of admiration, but you heard none of them. Coletto Negro was very proud.''

"Thank you Cabeza,'' I said simply and there were tears in my eyes. Neither of us spoke again for a while. I was grateful for the silence. It gave me time to control the emotions that were rising within me. I thought of Coletto Negro's pride in me. I thought also of my father. He had not been a coward. He had fought with nothing other than his hands in his attempt to protect my mother. If there had been more like him, things would have been different.

But there were not, so the situation remained forever unchanged. How I hated those Mexican weaklings.

Although I was unaware of it at the time, perhaps this was why I had experienced no strong feelings to return to my people. I was learning to become a man. Not just a man. But a being of courage and dignity. Life was no longer simply an existence. It was more. Much more. The Apaches were a proud race. They bowed before no one. They were very aggressive and cruel it is true. But never to their own people. Their standards of social behaviour were high and their strict moral code was rigidly adhered to by virtually everyone. The penalties for breaking it were harsh. For instance, a woman who was unfaithful to her husband ran the risk of having the tip of her nose cut off if her infidelity was discovered.

Among those virtues held in high esteem by the Apaches was speaking the truth. And to steal from members of their own tribe was considered a cardinal sin. They never failed to honour their debts and were generous to relatives and friends. In every band the weak were aided by the strong. The sick, bereaved, aged and disabled were all supported by their more fortunate comrades. And there was a great love among them for their children. Coletto Negro loved me as if I had been born his own son. He taught me how to be strong in mind and body, as did all Apache fathers teach their sons. And there was great satisfaction and enjoyment in the learning.

Perhaps these things were among the many thoughts that flitted in and out of my head as Cabeza and I sat there in contented reverie. Our daydreams were ended abruptly, however, by the sun which had sneaked unnoticed from behind the tall bushes that always gave my quiet place a degree of protection until almost noon.

"Ai-yee, it burns!" exclaimed Cabeza as he leaped frantically from his rocky seat; which had changed suddenly from pleasantly warm to uncomfortably hot.

"You are very observant my friend," I laughed. "If I had been able to move as fast this morning as you did just now then you would not have won the race."

"It is true," he agreed ruefully, rubbing his buttocks with both hands. "I think we should walk awhile. It is less painful than sitting."

We left the thicket and walked towards the stream where it would be cooler. "How long have you been with the Apaches?" asked Cabeza.

"More than one year although I do not know exactly. And

you?''

"Almost two years I think. It is difficult to be accurate. One can only judge by the seasons. I was ten years old when I was captured so I think I must be twelve now. How old are you?''

"Ten. They took me soon after my ninth birthday.''

We reached the stream and sat in the shadow of a large rock, with our feet dangling in the cool water. For a while we revelled in the tingling sensation of the current squeezing its way through the gaps separating our toes. We sat in silence, throwing pebbles at anything that moved; several lizards, a scorpion and a family of beetles industriously rolling in front of them a ball of mud several times as big as their largest member, a small rodent which disappeared as quickly as it arrived, and fish which leaped, open-mouthed, from the water to snap at the clouds of insects hovering leisurely above them. The soothing drone of thousands of minute wings and the happy ripple of frolicsome waters beneath. Ah, these were the sounds of childhood. Hear them again when you are older and hundred pleasant memories instantly invade your mind.

"Why do you not try to go back to Mexico?'' asked Cabeza suddenly.

His question caught me off-balance but I recovered quickly. "It is too far,'' I rationalized, "and I would probably lose myself in the desert. It is so big and I do not know in which direction to go. I have no horse or food. And if I did they would probably . . .''

"Slow down, fast-talking one. Slow down,'' interrupted Cabeza. "I think you do not tell me the truth. I think you like it here with the Apaches.''

"You are wrong. I do not . . .'' I stopped abruptly. It was bad to lie to a friend and I felt guilty and ashamed. "No. You are right. It is a better life here. These people are not slaves all their lives as we are in Mexico. They do not live in constant fear as we do. And my stomach is not so often empty here like it was there.''

"Your words make me feel much better Cuchillo. For a long time I hated the Apaches because of what they had done. But now I too like the road they travel. It is a dangerous road with hazards around almost every bend. But it is an exciting road. It is a man's road.''

I was surprised by Cabeza's words, but neither of us spoke again on the subject. What we had revealed to one another made the bond between us even stronger. It would take a lot to break it — and that was how it should be with true friends.

"You spoke of empty stomachs just now,'' said Cabeza lightly, beating his own like a war drum. "Mine is hollow and needs filling. Let us see what we can steal from the women of the village."

We both laughed, for the main meal of the day was eaten in the evening and to obtain food of substance at any other time resulted in a game enjoyed by all who participated. The women would pretend that we were not allowed anything at all, and then playfully curse us in mock anger when we took the food from under their noses. Still laughing, we both ran towards the village.

These were good times for the Apaches. Nearly all the American soldiers had been recalled to the east, where they were diligently butchering one another in the terrible civil war which had ripped the nation into two gigantic blood-drenched segments. Only a handful of men were left behind to protect the white settlers from Indian depredations. The Apaches struck whenever the mood took them, and wherever the plunder was choicest. For four years, until the end of the titanic struggle between North and South, these copper-coloured desert fighters reaped a horrible and bloody harvest throughout most of the Southwest. They became so confident that not even the larger settlements or towns were safe from attack.

# CHAPTER NINE

When we reached the camp the women were engaged in the preparation of various delicacies for the feast that would start as soon as their men returned from the hunt. All menial labour in an Apache society was done by the women. They cooked, carried, made clothes and even erected the homes in which they and their families lived. Yet they did it all without complaint. The role of the man encompassed but three tasks — fighting, stealing and hunting. His status within the band, and the overall unit of the tribe, depended upon his abilities to kill without being killed and to rob without being caught. Only in a chief was something more expected; the qualities of leadership, diplomacy, strategy, intellect and unwavering resolution.

The women were preparing the food in the open as was customary. One fat old crone of many summers, and countless nights judging by the large number of children she had, winked at an untidy heap of ancient bones and wrinkled flesh seated beside her. Both of them began to speak in stage whispers. We pretended not to hear, and strolled nonchalantly among the women as they worked tirelessly under a tireless sun. The air was dry, yet our mouths were moist at the thought of sinking our teeth into any one of the many appetizing dishes spread on the ground.

We stopped in front of a grey-haired women who was busily turning out acorn meal cakes. These were a particular favourite among young children. "Go away," scolded the women in mock severity, shaking a fist at us. The others around her grinned and we moved on. But only a few yards. This time to a pretty girl of no more than twenty years who was but recently married. On the ground in front of her was a quantity of freshly-roasted mescal, the bread of the Apaches. Cabeza bent low, his hands reaching down. She was obviously embarrassed but played her part nonetheless. "Leave them alone, thief."

"You misjudge me pretty one," said Cabeza in an injured tone. "It was my intention merely to adjust the toe of my moccasin which was paining me. And not to take, without invitation, this delicious food prepared by your own sweet hands."

The other women laughed loudly. Even the young one, despite her discomfort, could not prevent a smile pushing up the corners of her mouth. Cabeza had a way with words and, for one so young, a way with the opposite sex. At that moment I do believe he could have taken whatever dish he fancied without any attempt being made to stop him. But he continued to play the game and walked a few paces more. I followed him. The women bent their heads as if they were working, but they were only awaiting our next move.

This time it was mine. The attention of the women was rivetted upon Cabeza, now on his knees in front of a batch of mesquite bean meal cakes, sniffing intently at their delicate aroma. With both hands I silently and quickly scooped up a large earthenware bowl, filled with dried fruit of the cactus, and started running. I had taken several steps before our subterfuge was fully realized. There were many shouts of "Stop thief!" but there would be no pursuit. The game was ended and the women would continue with their preparations while laughingly discussing our cunning manoeuvre.

Cabeza and I did not stop running, however, until we found a shaded area where we could sit and eat in comfort. The fruit was delicious. The Apaches harvested it from several species of cactus. When dried, such fruit tasted much like bananas, figs and dates.

Like all Apache boys I had developed into an expert swimmer with a great love of the water, so I suggested to Cabeza that we pass an hour or so in the stream.

"I do not feel like swimming. My stomach is too heavy with the fruit you so wickedly stole," he replied. Silence for several seconds, then: "I tell you what would be better Cuchillo. To walk slowly in any direction you choose until our stomachs feel lighter. Then, from whatever point we have reached, to run without stopping to the swimming hole where we will laze in the water for as long as we wish."

"That is an excellent idea. It is reassuring for one to learn that his friend is not as stupid as he looks."

"You are right," sighed Cabeza. "And so much more fortunate than I am. For I have a friend who is even less intelligent than he appears, if that is possible."

Despite his professed handicap of an inside weighed down with food, Cabeza was soon beyond the range of the rocks I hurled after him. After halting briefly to make a derisive gesture with his buttocks he immediately resumed his deceptive stride, ugly but undeniably effective. The distance between us increased rapidly. "Oh no," I groaned to myself. "Not again today. So much for our leisurely stroll." And I sprinted after him.

It is said that to be a great runner you must first suffer hunger. This was certainly true for us. In less than a mile we were exhausted. Cabeza collapsed first and I followed suit the instant I reached him. He was rolling on the sun-baked earth, holding his stomach in feigned agony. Exaggerated groans disturbed the area's tranquility. "I am dying Cuchillo," he gasped. "Go on without me. Save yourself from the sun's terrible heat and the almost endless desert that stretches before you. Do not worry about me. At least I shall die bravely."

"For someone who is at the gates of death you take far too long to enter," I replied unsympathetically, sprawled breathlessly a few feet from him. "You talk too much for a person whose condition demands that he should treat breathing as a luxury soon to be taken from him."

He pushed himself to a kneeling position. "Your grief overwhelms me. Never have I had such a friend. Concern yourself no further. For your sake alone I will fight and conquer this sickness which has stricken me."

"Do not undertake so prodigious a struggle for one as unworthy of our efforts as I am. Just relax and die quietly. I will shoulder my sorrow like a man should."

"So be it. You wish me recovered and I am immediately well again. It is a miracle."

Fearing that further insults would provoke retaliation and result in an energy-sapping tussle which my weakened stamina could ill afford, I hastily turned the conversation in another direction. "You have forgotten our walk. There is a high butte several miles south of here which I have long wanted to climb. But it is a difficult ascent to attempt without a sturdy companion. What do you say?"

"I agree but with a condition that we still enjoy a swim when the climb is finished. Or perhaps you do not have the strength for all this."

"I have the strength so long as you do not collapse and cause me to carry you the rest of the way."

"So be it. But this time we will not race. It is difficult for me to converse with you when you are always so far behind."

Allowing him the final words in our verbal battle I trotted leisurely away. He loped easily alongside. As the distance passed steadily beneath our feet we spoke little. Most of the time I was thinking about this new life to which we had so quickly adapted ourselves. Born into two opposing forms of civilized society, one democratic, the other autocratic, we now lived in contented harmony within the bounds of a single primitive unit. Why had we accepted the change so readily? And we were not alone in this transition. Grown men had deliberately turned their backs on civilization and were now Indians in all but the colour of their skin. These were from among the trappers, mountain men, pathfinders and traders. Was it the complete independence of life and movement which attracted them? Or the absolute security of tribal unity? Perhaps a combination of both. It was also possible that they . . .

Cabeza brought all further conjecture and movement to an abrupt halt by grabbing my arm. "Look," he said tersely, pointing to our right. "Is that not the chief's horse?" It was. Easily recognizable because of its vivid brown and white markings and long flowing white tail, it stood about a half-mile distant. Its head was close to the ground in a grazing attitude. But not even the hardiest Indian pony could subsist on a diet of sand and rock and that is all there was for at least a mile around. We moved closer.

"Perhaps it has broken free from the village herd," I suggested. "Pablo Azul would be very grateful if we recaptured it for him as he prizes it greatly." As we drew nearer, Cabeza moved wordlessly to the right and I stealthily approached it from the left. Suddenly we stopped as one. The animal was not grazing. Its head was held low by a brown hand entangled in the pony's bridle-strap. The hand protruded from a small group of almost flat boulders that rose less than two feet from the desert floor. We moved forward again but now we were running.

It was Pablo Azul. His head was squashed tight against one of the low rocks which had concealed him from us. His face was covered in blood and his neck was broken. He smelled strongly of whisky and there was an almost empty bottle a few yards back.

For perhaps a minute we stood there silently. I remember thinking: "This is no way for an Apache chief to die. A warrior who goes before his natural time should be killed by shots from a gun, not from a bottle." But a fatal weakness among far too many Indians was their love of liquor, particularly whisky. Where the white man's firearms failed, his firewater often succeeded.

Cabeza broke the silence. "What shall we do?" he asked simply.

"We must tie his body to his pony and return him to the village," I replied. "They will do what has to be done."

The dead chief was fat and heavy. Almost too heavy for two slightly built boys. But with a final concerted effort we had him lying on his stomach across the horse's back and tied him in position with a length of the bridle-strap. As we led the animal slowly in the direction of the village I stared in morbid fascination at the chief's lifeless head as it rolled grotesquely from side to side in rhythm with the horse's gait.

# CHAPTER TEN

There was an eerie silence as we walked the mount and its gruesome burden through the groups of women; no longer working contentedly but frozen into immobile curiosity. We stopped outside the wickiup of the village medicine man, Juan Caballo. He would know what to do. He was as old and wise as time itself. Neither of us had the courage to enter his lodge or to call him. In Apache society the aged were treated with great respect. With the medicine man, or shaman, this amounted almost to reverence.

The old man must have sensed the abnormal atmosphere that now existed throughout the camp, perhaps it was the sudden absence of the women's happy banter, for within a few minutes he shuffled into the sunlight. His movements were slow, painfully so, and his dried-up face was criss-crossed with lines like so many cracks covering the surface of eroded rock. Only his mind remained young. Its vitality was reflected in his eyes which missed nothing. He moved closer to the chief's body and his nostrils wrinkled in disgust. He shook his head sadly.

"Too drunk to stay on his horse," he muttered. "Something like this was bound to happen. If not today, then later. Perhaps it is best this way. He had ceased to be an Apache long ago in all but his birthright." His voice became louder. "But he was a chief and he will be buried as such." He turned to us. "Stay here. I will make the arrangements."

Apaches were among the deadliest killers to be found anywhere in the world — and yet they were forever terrified by the proximity of the dead. For this reason corpses were always interred with the least possible delay. Generally during daylight on the day the person died. The body was prepared for burial by the closest male relatives. In this case it was Pablo Azul's younger brother and their ancient father who performed the unwelcome task. The dead chief's brother had not joined the deer-hunting party that morning. He would never go on another hunt or raid, for he had been horribly crippled by a rifle bullet during a foray into Mexico a few years previously. One leg was now crooked and several inches shorter than the other. He moved only with great difficulty. The three men approached us. Only the shaman spoke. The others remained impassive. It was the Apache way not to display emotion, only to feel it inside.

"Follow us with the horse," he said quietly. "We shall have need of your young strength."

As the trio moved off slowly we joined the end of the

pathetically small funeral procession. Pablo Azul's father spoke to an old man who was passing. He changed direction and, despite his age, trotted towards the dead chief's wickiup.

After walking at a slow pace for almost an hour, we came to a deep crack in the earth's surface. Here we stopped. The crevice was little wider than the height of an average man and only thirty to forty yards long. I leaned over and looked down, but all I could see was an impenetrable blackness.

Juan Caballo looked at Pablo Azul's father who nodded in return. "This will suffice," he said. His voice was tired. He was a weary old man and I suddenly felt sorry for him. His son could have been a great chief. Instead he had died a drunkard. His only other son was permanently deformed. One had been crippled mentally, the other physically. Between them they would not have made a whole man. No one left to perpetuate the exploits of a man who, in his prime, had led his people on countless successful sorties against the Navajos, Comanches, Kiowas, Mexicans and the ever-encroaching Anglo-Americans.

No words were spoken as the old man and his son laboriously eased the flabby bulk of Pablo Azul's body from the horse. With the help of the shaman, they lowered the corpse gently to the ground. Cabeza and I stood back respectfully. We did not offer assistance. If they wanted our aid they would ask for it. Such was the custom.

The crippled-one took a razor-edged knife from the top of his moccasin and, with one deft stroke, slit the horse's throat. Blood spurted from the wound and the pony's legs buckled beneath it. As soon as it had twitched itself into a final stillness there on the earth, now blotched dark red around the lifeless animal, the crippled-one looked towards us and pointed with his knife at the narrow cleft in the ground. We knew what to do. It was an Apache tradition to bury the personal effects of the deceased together with the body.

The dead pony was a great weight. But the crevice was only a few feet away and, with the crippled-one's assistance, we dragged its body to the edge and tumbled it into the blackness. It struck the bottom long before I had anticipated it would, so the hole was not as deep as it had at first appeared. This was good because the chief's body would have to be lowered the entire distance; not merely thrown in as would be the case with all his property when it arrived.

We sat and waited. After perhaps an hour the old man, to whom Pablo Azul's father had spoken in the village, arrived leading a horse dragging travois; two light poles attached to the rear of the horse with their other ends trailing on the ground. Loaded on the travois were all the dead man's possessions. There were buffalo robes, brilliantly coloured Navajo blankets, his ceremonial attire, an elaborately decorated war lance, bow and arrow and a beautifully engraved shotgun with twin barrels of gleaming silver. It seemed a terrible waste to bury such a magnificent weapon. One after another the articles were dropped into the pit. Ropes were taken from the travois, looped around Pablo Azul's legs and chest, and slowly his body was lowered into the crevice. As soon as it touched the bottom Juan Caballo ordered us to push as much dirt, brush and rocks as we could into the hole, so that no animals or birds of carrion could mutilate the corpse. It was back-breaking work; but Cabeza and I did not stop until we were commanded to do so.

Before starting the return journey to the village, the crippled-one removed the travois from the horse that had brought his brother's personal belongings to the burial place, and handed me the reins. "Ride out and meet the hunting party. They will be returning from the mountains. Tell them what has happened."

The pony was a large, mettlesome dun. It was in a frisky mood and I mounted it only with great difficulty. But this was not a time for laughter and no one ridiculed my efforts. Once firmly in the saddle I felt the horse move smoothly and swiftly beneath me. In less than two hours I saw the hunters. They were returning to the camp just as the crippled-one had stated. Their packhorses were laden with fresh meat. As the men drew nearer I could hear them laughing and shouting. The hunt and obviously been a good one. Coletto Negro beckoned me to him with one huge sweep of his arm.

"Slow down fast-riding one or your mount will die before his time," he commented as I breathlessly reined the pony to a leisurely canter alongside his own horse. "What is your hurry? Do the evil spirits chase you? Or are you running away to Mexico? If so it is in the opposite direction to the one you are taking." The others laughed loudly for they all knew he was joking. Coletto Negro laughed also but stopped almost immediately.

"Your face is too serious Cuchillo," he observed. "Why is this? Tonight there will be much feasting and your stomach will be filled with the choicest cuts of venison. This is no time for sadness."

"There will be no feasting tonight my father," I replied.

Coletto Negro jerked his horse to a standstill. "What is this? Is there something wrong at the village?" The other riders clustered around us.

"The chief is dead," I told them simply. A few seconds silence, followed by a hubbub of voices.

"Quiet!" thundered Coletto Negro. "How did it happen?" he asked. "A fight with the Mexicans? An accident?"

"Yes. It was an accident."

"But how?"

"He was drunk and fell from his horse. His hand caught in the reins and he was dragged to death."

Without further speech Coletto Negro dug his heels viciously into his horse's flanks and galloped towards the camp. The others followed in absolute silence. I rode at the very rear.

As we entered the village the last few defiant flames were spluttering among the final remains of the chief's wickiup. It was the custom to burn a dead man's home and its contents immediately following his death. All those concerned with destroying the lodge and burying Pablo Azul were then required by tradition to burn their own clothes and purify their bodies with the smoke of sagebrush. This included Cabeza and myself. Also, according to custom, a dead man's dependents had to build a fresh lodge in another area of the village as soon as the burial ceremony was complete. Pablo Azul had left no children. Only a widow whose rolls of fat bounced as she walked. The other women helped her construct a new wickiup. And Pablo Azul's name was heard no more for it was forbidden to speak of the dead or visit their graves.

That night the old men and warriors of the village sat around the council fire to select a new leader. The following morning I learned that their choice was Coletto Negro. I was the son of a chief. My chest swelled with pride.

# CHAPTER ELEVEN

A short time before noon the sun-baked earth reverberated to the pounding of horses' hooves as more than fifty armed and mounted warriors, streaked with paint, reined their sweating ponies to a standstill in the village centre. Astride his war horse my father awaited their coming. Both he and the golden-brown pony appeared as a life-size statue carved in bronze. Beside him stood the ancient medicine man, Juan Caballo. My father held his right arm aloft for silence. It was an exhilarating, and somewhat fearsome, spectacle. I saw everything from the shady entrance to Cabeza's lodge where we had both been seated discussing our plans for the afternoon.

Coletto Negro adressed the now quietened warriors. He spoke with dignity, with solemnity and with emotion. "The shaman has had a vision," he said. "In that dream he saw many pony soldiers. There was much fighting and killing. And when the fighting and killing was finished many of us were dead. The rest were taken as prisoners to a distant land where they died from sickness and starvation."

There was instant uproar, for this shaman was a renowned prophet. Medicine men were always beings of great spiritual prowess. Some were healers of the sick, some controlled the creatures of the wild places, some were bringers of rain and others exercised miraculous protective powers. But the seers who could also interpret the omens they experienced; for them was reserved the greatest respect of all.

Coletto Negro signalled for silence again and the hubbub subsided immediately. "But in his dream the shaman also saw those who guided the soldiers to our village. The Mexicans from the copper mines. They were the ones who brought them."

"But why should they do this thing?" asked one of the assembled warriors. I recognized Lobo's voice. "We have never harmed them. They have been permitted to live and mine in peace."

This time it was Juan Caballo who spoke. "They are afraid of us. Their protector among us is now dead. They fear that without his restraining influence we will drive them from our lands. From the places where they grow rich by digging holes in the ground for the metal they desire so much. But the earth is mother to the Apache people. It is a sin to mutilate our mother or to allow anyone else to do so. The Mexicans know how we think. They can no longer buy protection with whisky. So they will now look to the pony soldiers and their guns for help. They will guide them here. And when it is all finished this place will be as their own. Before they can do this we must send them away forever." He looked up at Coletto Negro. Now all eyes were upon the new chief.

His words came slowly and deliberately. "Juan Caballo speaks a great truth," he said. "In their own country these Mexicans would be our enemies. Do we not frequently raid their countrymen to the south for the many things we need in order to live? So why should these people be as our friends in this land which does not belong to them? Why should they despoil the earth which is our mother?" A few seconds silence as he studied carefully the faces of the Apaches as they awaited his decision.

"We will ride down to the mines now and tell them to leave. They will be given one day. There will be no fighting, no blood will be spilled, if they are gone in this time. But if not, then there will be war. Come." He wheeled his pony in a semi-circle and rode down towards the mines. The warriors followed, the sunlight winking on the barrels of their rifles with which most were armed. Only a few carried bows and arrows. Those with rifles also had well-filled ammunition bandoliers slung across their shoulders.

"Cuchillo!" Cabeza's voice was low and urgent. "Let us take the swift way down. We can reach the bottom before the horses. Then, if we hide in the brush, we will see everything."

"But . . ."

"This is no time for hesitation," Cabeza interrupted impatiently. "Are you afraid?"

"No."

"Then come."

We slithered down the rock face with the assurance of mountain goats. It was a path we both knew well, having employed it on numerous occasions to watch the Mexicans at work in and around the mines. Breathless and excited, we arrived at the rock base several minutes before the first pony, that of my father, came into view. We were well concealed in the thick bushes that skirted the mines and no one saw us.

The sound of so many horses brought the miners, ragged and dirty, tumbling from the mines like so many gophers disturbed from their holes by a family of irate rattlesnakes. They looked so frightened that I regarded them solely with contempt. Once they had been my people but I no longer felt any sentiment for them. Not even pity. They just stood there, nervously rubbing the soles of their sandals or bare feet against the ground and the dust arose like a fine white powder. Around them the Apaches slowly rode their ponies like cowboys herding cattle. Except that the cattle were sheep.

Superficially, there was little difference physically between the Apaches and the Mexicans. Their hair was black, their eyes dark brown and their skins the colour of copper. They even smelled the same. Sweaty and dirty. Although dissimilar in design their apparel was generally of the same inferior quality. No, the only real difference was in their bearing. And that came from within. The Apaches were proud and fiery. The Mexicans were downtrodden and spiritless.

Suddenly the door of a nearby adobe structure was thrown open and three men strode out. Two of them, both neatly-attired, were the mine-owners. The third, in a soiled linen suit that was once white, was the foreman. One of the owners, a huge man with a cigar poking out from beneath a drooping moustache, shouted across at the miners: "Who told you to stop work? Return to the mines!"

A few of the Mexican labourers made a half-hearted attempt to break through the circle of mounted warriors but were instantly pushed back. And there they remained. Small beads of sweat appeared on their foreheads. But it was not the perspiration which comes with heat or hard work. It was that which comes with fear.

"Where is your chief?" the Mexican with the cigar asked the Apaches now closing in on him as well.

"I am here," replied Coletto Negro simply.

The cigar fell from the fat man's gaping mouth. "But you are not Pablo Azul. Where is he?"

"He is no more. Your whisky killed him. I have been chosen to lead in his place. And I do not like whisky." His voice was instantly ominous. "Neither do I like those who despoil land which is not their land but which belongs to the people who have selected me as their chief." He pointed skywards. "The sun is now at its highest point. When it reaches the same position tomorrow you will all be gone from this place. Or die here."

"But this is our property," protested the other mine-owner, as fat as his partner but without a moustache. "These are our mines. We have worked them for years. Our homes are here. If you think that . . ."

"I think nothing," interrupted the Chiricahua leader fiercely. "I know. And what I know is that this is our country. And if you are still here one day from now then we will kill you. Not one of you will be left alive. And the dying will not be easy or quick."

The man without the moustache deflated immediately. "Can

we not discuss this?'' he pleaded, mopping his forehead with a white kerchief. ''Perhaps there is an alternative.''

''We have discussed it and I have given you your choice. Return to Mexico with your lives as gifts from us. Or remain here and we will take them from you.'' He reined his mount viciously in a half-circle and returned the way he had come. The other Chiricahuas did likewise.

Throughout the afternoon and evening a multitude of noises drifted upwards from the mining settlement. There was a constant bustle. Wagons creaked as they were hastily loaded. Men shouted orders and cursed one another. Dogs barked. Women called frantically to their children. Horses were harnessed to wagons. And finally, the plodding sound of horses' hooves followed closely by the screeching of wheels turning on dry axles.

By noon the following day the settlement was completely deserted. Apart from the Apaches, men, women and children, who had swooped down from our village like a swarm of locusts to denude the area of everything useful or ornamental which the Mexicans had left behind during their hasty departure.

Coletto Negro did not go down. He just stood on the edge of the escarpment looking thoughtfully into the distance. He heard the laughter of his people ransacking the settlement below but his eyes saw far beyond them. Lobo stood beside him. I watched them both.

''You are concerned my chief,'' said Lobo quietly. ''You feel that these Mexicans may tell the pony soldiers of our camp here on the mesa as revenge for sending them from their mines and homes.''

''It is possible. I have considered it a great deal. But the white-eyes are still fighting each other in the east and the few that remain behind do so only to protect their own kind from raids by our people. Not to attack us. I do not think they will trouble us if we leave them alone and fight only the Mexicans whom they despise almost as much as we do. No, my good friend, I fear for the time when the white-eye soldiers stop killing one another and come looking for us again. They are great warriors and more numerous than fleas on a dog.''

# CHAPTER TWELVE

April 9, 1865. The American Civil War ended after four years of bitter and bloody fighting when General Robert E. Lee, commanding the South, finally surrendered to his counterpart from the North, General Ulysses S. Grant, at Appomattox Court House.

Most of the men who had been engaged in the struggle were glad to leave the army and attempt to salvage something of their former lives. But not all. For many the army had become a way of life. It provided a home, comradeship and a regular, if somewhat inadequate, source of income. In short, a regular job laced with travel and excitement for those who were restless and hated to remain in any one place for very long. This was not a bad thing for the United States Army. It needed such men, even during times of comparative peace.

But there were other types. The glory-seekers and power-hungry. Men like the notorious George Armstrong Custer, brevetted a major general in the Union Army for his outstanding heroics on the battlefields of the east, who suddenly found himself reduced to a mere lieutenant colonel in the regular army immediately the Civil War was over. Such men came west after war in an attempt to regain lost rank and prestige by deliberately inciting the Indians to violence, and then leading campaigns against them. Not all officers who came west were of Custer's calibre. But there were more than enough of his kind to ensure the Indians a most unhealthy future. The Chiricahua Apaches never fought against Custer. Whatever ambitions he may have entertained were curtailed forever by the Sioux and Cheyenne in 1876 at the battle of the Little Big Horn during which his entire command was annihilated.

Another such man who rode westward with bitterness eating into his soul like a cancer was Major, formerly Brevet Brigadier General, Jefferson Glencoe. Our first encounrter with him was late in 1865. I was eleven, or perhaps twelve, years old. Cabeza and I were walking along the rim of a precipitous canyon four or five miles from the village. Looking down, we suddenly saw a long line of United States troopers winding its way along the tortuous bottom of the canyon like some gigantic blue and yellow snake. The file of cavalrymen seemed without end. As one we both dropped to the ground and, lying on our stomachs, peered over the edge of the great rift.

"Ai-yee," breathed Cabeza in awe. "Never before have I seen so many pony soldiers at one time."

"They also have many weapons," I whispered, noting that

each man carried a rifle in a saddle holster, a revolver strapped to the right of his waist and a saber to the left. "These men are equipped to fight. But who? Why are there so many of them?"

"There has been talk in the village that the war in the east is no more. These soldiers look for Indians I think, perhaps our own people." Cabeza's voice became urgent. "We must warn them."

Easing our way quietly back from the canyon rim, we commenced the long run back to the camp. It was the most important race of our lives. And, I think, the toughest. The sharp rocks cut through our moccasins and our feet were soon caked with dust turned to red by our own blood. We ran swiftly, side by side, each drawing strength from the presence of the other. On this occasion time alone was our rival. But we did not speak. There was sufficient breath only for the long distance ahead.

We stumbled into the camp just as Coletto Negro was preparing to lead a hunting party into the mountains. But he saw us and jerked his pony to a standstill. The rest followed suit. They all knew something was wrong. Our condition told them so.

"What is it my son?" the chief asked tersely as I grasped the stirrup of his mount.

"Pony soldiers!" was all I could say. My lungs felt as if they were filled with live coals.

"How many?"

I was too breathless to answer. Instead it was Cabeza's voice which replied. "Two hundred," he gasped. "Perhaps more."

A murmur, like the buzz of angry bees when their hive has been disturbed, ran through the assembled hunting party.

"How distant?" demanded Coletto Negro. There was an urgency now in his questions.

This time I answered. "Four or five miles when we first saw them. Two or three now I would think. They were not travelling fast and it is difficult country."

Lobo spoke. "How are they armed?" he asked.

"Each man carries a rifle, revolver and saber," I told him.

"And I am certain I saw many pack-mules at the rear carrying boxes of ammunition," added Cabeza. "They come prepared for battle."

"Then it is true," sighed Coletto Negro in weary resignation. "They have finished fighting among themselves. Now they come to make war with us as before. So be it. We will be ready for them. It is lucky for us that you observed them when you did."

"And fortunate that we had not left already for the hunt," added Lobo, "or the village would have been defenceless."

Including the young apprentice warriors, Coletto Negro had a total fighting force of approximately eighty men. Less than half the number of pony soldiers; but more than enough to defend the village which, hid among the rocks, was a natural fortress. There was abundant drinking water from the stream and we had plenty of food. Under these conditions the chief felt confident that we could hold off any attack longer than the other force involved could afford to besiege us. Of necessity their supplies would be severely limited.

With swift sweeping movements of his right arm and a few sharp commands, Coletto Negro deployed his men like the trained fighting leader he was. To the rear of the village was a large depression, in the middle of a tall upthrust of rock, which afforded protection from any bullets fired from below. Into this hollow were herded the women and children. To our disgust these included Cabeza and me. But a boy was not permitted to become an apprentice warrior until he was at least fifteen.

The fighting men, at the chief's instructions, broke up into groups of from six to ten men. Each party concealed itself behind evenly spaced ramparts of boulders. These had been constructed many years before for just such an occasion as the one which was now approaching. Small gaps had been left among the boulders to give those warriors protected by them a maximum view of the country below and wide, unobstructed areas of fire.

Once in position we did not have long to wait. After half an hour or so, the leading men of the column were sighted by a sharp-eyed young brave who called out to the others: ''They are here. To the left.''

Hearing his words and not wishing to miss any of the promised excitement, Cabeza and I crept unnoticed from among the women and children and silently found a vantage point close to the warriors, yet where they could not see us. I looked around. None of our people were exposed to the oncoming troopers. Each was crouched low behind the fortifications like a mountain lion patiently awaiting its prey. I felt exalted and confident. The soldiers would be defeated if there was a battle.

As they came steadily closer I could see the pony soldier chief clearly. He was a tall man, upright in his saddle, but with a large paunch. His face was red from the desert sun and he had a thick black beard. When five or six hundred yards off he raised his right arm high in the air and his men drew their mounts to a halt. Further signals and they wheeled their horses into four long ranks behind him. It was an impressive sight. The pack-mules, together

41

with five wagons I had not noticed before, remained at the rear.

Another factor, of which Cabeza and I had been completely unaware when we first saw the pony soldiers in the canyon, was the presence of a small company of Indian scouts. These were from among the Maricopa, Papago and Pima tribes, all hereditary enemies of the Apache people. I heard several of our braves spit contemptuously as soon as they noticed the scouts swing out from behind the cavalrymen and position themselves on the right flank.

The soldier chief rode forward with two other soldiers. One had a set of three yellow marks, all shaped as the fork of a snake's tongue, on each sleeve. The other had a wide yellow line across each shoulder of his jacket. The one with three yellow forks on his sleeves carried a long stick with a piece of white cloth hanging from the top. The remainder of the soldiers stayed in formation.

The three men halted at the base of the rocks — where we were all positioned — dismounted and waited. They carried no weapons.

Discerning movements to my right, I looked across and saw my father descending the rock face together with Lobo and another warrior whose name I did not know. They also were unarmed. At the bottom of the steep slope they stopped within a few yards of the three soldiers.

What I am about to tell you I can do so only because Cabeza knew the white-eye language and translated for me all that transpired.

The soldier chief turned to the man with the yellow forks on his sleeves. "I knew they were here," he said triumphantly. "Fetch the Pima interpreter, sergeant." All this time his right arm was held aloft, palm outwards, in the sign of peace.

As the sergeant remounted, Lobo spoke. "No need stinking Pima. Speak your tongue. Many years ago white trader teach. No forget. Speak good."

The soldier-leader lowered his arm and half-turned. "All right sergeant. As you were."

His commanding officer now addressed Lobo. "I am Major Glencoe. Are you chief of this tribe?" he asked.

"No. Him chief. Name Coletto Negro," replied Lobo, indicating my father.

"Tell your chief that I come from the great white father in Washington," said the major.

Lobo spoke to Coletto Negro in Apache and then translated the chief's reply to Major Glencoe. "Chief say father not white. Same colour him. Say not in place you say. Say died many years ago. Buried in mountains three days journey from village."

The major breathed deeply to control his anger. "I did not mean father in that sense. I refer to the great white father who is chief of all Indians. And Americans."

A brief conversation with Coletto Negro, then Lobo spoke again to the major. "Him say great white father chief all Americans maybe. Not chief all Indians. Indians have many chiefs. But not one white. Coletto Negro our chief. Him not white."

Major Glencoe exploded. "You tell whatever he calls himself that the big white chief is far greater than he is. That he has terrible powers." His voice grew louder and his face redder. "You tell him that this land on which his tribe now lives belongs to the great white father and that he has ordered your people to go to the reservation at Bosque Redondo. That is why I am here. To take you there. By force if necessary. You tell him that."

Lobo translated all this to Coletto Negro who listened impassively and then answered abruptly.

Lobo interpreted. "Him say no leave here. Like country very much. No go Bosque Redondo. Too far east. Is Navajo reservation. Mescalero Apaches sent there one time by white-eye soldiers. All time fighting Navajos. Too many Navajos so Mescaleros leave. We stay here. Chief say you want fight then you got fight."

With these words the three Chiricahuas turned and started the long walk back up the slope. The pony soldier chief stood speechless with anger for a few seconds. Then he blurted out in uncontrolled rage. "You insolent bastards. I'll make it so hot for you up there that you'll come crawling back down, begging for mercy."

Lobo suddenly turned round and strode back. The other two continued climbing the rock face. The major was remounting his horse when Lobo called out. "Glencoe!" he shouted. "You wait short time."

The soldier chief climbed down again and waited. His hands were clenching and unclenching in an effort to restrain the terrible temper rising within him. Lobo stopped a few inches in front of the major who was considerably taller than the stocky Apache.

Lobo's voice was low but clear. "This time Glencoe I do not speak for chief. Only me. White trader teach me your tongue good man. Teach me many things. Tell me when talk with any man look at eyes. Truth not always in words, always in eyes. I watch your eyes Glencoe. You not want peace with us. You want fight. So I tell you now. I kill you first chance." With these words he turned and followed his leader and the other warrior who were already half-way up the rocky slope.

Major Glencoe climbed back on his horse in frustrated silence. He turned to the soldier with yellow lines on his shoulders. "Let's go lieutenant!" he barked. "No ignorant savage talks to me that way. Never! I'll teach the bastards!" The sergeant followed them. He did not speak. His craggy face was thoughtful, even serious. Unlike his superiors he knew that this was going to be far more than a mere carnival of fireworks. He knew there would be much killing and that many soldiers would die. While his commanding officer had been busy with words he had not. I had seen him looking up at our defences. He had noted the huge sturdy walls of boulders behind which our men were positioned. He had seen the many rifle barrels protruding from among those same boulders.

# CHAPTER THIRTEEN

Immediately Coletto Negro regained the top he called together his most experienced fighting men for a brief talk. That war with the pony soldiers was imminent there was no doubt. But there was a great confidence among our warriors. The shaman had consulted the omens and had forecast a great victory for us. Our men were all armed with rifles, most of them of the latest type, and ammunition was plentiful. Unscrupulous American traders had been more than eager to exchange such weapons and ammunition for the herds of horses and cattle which the Apaches brought back from their periodic marauding into Mexico.

Our fighting men also knew that even if the troopers below were to receive further supplies to augment their obviously limited resources, no number of bullets could conquer the weather. The cold hand of winter was slowly reaching out across this big land and soon the entire area would be caught firmly in its icy grasp. Even now the days were growing shorter and the nights colder. So cold that no Apache slept without thick buffalo robes covering his body and a fire burning in the centre of his wickiup. The sun, changed from summer's fiery whiteness to the pale yellow of early winter, was already commencing the long descent to its nightly resting place beyond the mountains. In a few hours the land would be covered by darkness. Then the earth would freeze until the sun returned to warm it again. In the morning we would see whether these white-eye soldiers still displayed the same eagerness to fight which they now showed.

Then one word, which came clearly across the distance separating us from the cavalry, severely dented our complacency. The voice was that of Major Glencoe. "Artillery!" he roared. From behind the wagons smaller groups of soldiers dragged three huge guns mounted on wheels.

"Wagon guns!" hissed a warrior close by. "We are lost."

Coletto Negro, a few yards away, must have heard him. He turned towards the man. "We are not lost." He spat the words with vehemence. "Even the great bullets from those big guns cannot penetrate our defences where the rocks are thickest. We must leave the weaker ramparts and fight from behind only the strongest. Come."

Those warriors manning the smaller barricades at once regrouped with their comrades already stationed behind the larger fortifications. Undetected, Cabeza and I rejoined the women and children. I felt fear in my stomach. The size of the wagon guns was unbelievable. Never before had I seen guns of such magnitude.

"Fire!" Major Glencoe's command was as distinct to us as it must have been to his own men. The three massive cannons spoke in unison and smoke belched from their gaping mouths. But the shells which landed in our rocky fortress were not the same type experienced years before by the seasoned warriors. These shells exploded on impact and fragments of metal hurtled in all directions. None of us were struck during this open bombardment, but one or two horses shrilled with pain as metal pieces tore into them.

"Take those ponies further back!" shouted Coletto Negro. two fledgling braves of no more than sixteen years rushed from behind the barricades to herd the horses to a safer position.

A crackle of small arms fire from below to keep our heads down while the cannons were being reloaded. But Coletto Negro's voice could be heard clearly, and coolly, above the noise. "The soldier chief is a fool. He fires all his big guns at one time instead of each following the other. So when the wagon guns speak everyone keep low. But after the big bullets have burst against the rocks we will shoot at the pony soldiers while they reload the wagon guns. We are well protected and not easy to see behind these rocks so their rifle fire will trouble us little." He named several warriors, all known to be excellent shots, to pick off the men operating the cannons. The remainder of our fighting men were to concentrate their fire on the long ranks of kneeling soldiers.

"Fire!" The cannons roared as one for a second time. Then came again the staccato sound of the troopers' rifles. But this time our men answered with their own weapons. Soldiers reloading the big guns crumpled to the ground. Some crawled painfully towards the nearest cover. Some lay, calling for help, where they had fallen. Others never made a sound or moved again. As the men fell so others were ordered forward to replace them. But our marksmen cut most of them down before they reached the guns. Those who made it were dropped by Apache bullets soon afterwards.

Our warriors were jubilant. The fieldpieces were immobilized. The battle was reduced to sporadic bursts of rifle fire from both sides, with our people steadily creating gaps in the opposition. Having relied solely upon the surprise and superiority of their field guns, the enemy had neglected to select good defensive positions. Now those same big guns were inactive, the pony soldiers were paying the penalty and their ranks were being cut slowly to pieces.

Then it happened. The horses were cut loose from the five wagons, which were then pushed steadily forward by troopers clustered behind them. Within minutes the wagons were level with the cannons and so manoeuvred that a wagon now flanked each gun. This afforded excellent protection for the soldiers who lost no time in reloading and operating the artillery.

The situation was now completely reversed. They had readjusted the range of the cannons so that the shells cleared the tops of our barricades and exploded behind them. The splinters of flying metal were everywhere. Many men were hit. Several of our bravest fighters were down with fragments embedded in their bodies. Some were writhing in pain, the earth around them dark-stained with slowly spreading patches of blood.

Although these were our first casualties of the battle, the wounds inflicted were so hideous that it was easy to detect a rapidly increasing panic among the defenders. They were not used to this type of warfare. The explosive missiles continued to shriek overhead. The warriors were now considerably unsettled and confused. A disorderly flight appeared imminent for here were weapons with which they could not contend. The shells were falling with terrifying accuracy and regularity. The air was filled with the confused sounds of explosions, men screaming with instant pain or groaning in prolonged agony, the wailing of the women for their menfolk as they fell and children screaming and weeping in absolute terror. The carnage was horrible.

"Retreat to the council rocks!" Coletto Negro's voice was loud, yet calm and decisive. His command came immediately following a bombardment of shells. The warriors took advantage of the brief lull, caused by the pony soldiers reloading the fieldpieces, to collect their wounded comrades and withdraw to the rocks indicated by their leader.

The council rocks formed an impregnable area in the centre of the village. They were so called because this was where the important men of the band held council. Here they discussed and formulated the policies that had kept us free, while other Apaches were penned on reservations like so many wild horses and cattle. The rocks formed an almost complete circle. They were so thick that no shell could breach them and it would have taken an artillery genius to drop the explosive missiles through the narrow opening at the top. But there was one severe limitation. The council rocks contained no positions from which to return fire.

Everyone, including women and children, were now huddled in this narrow confine which protected us from further injury as the shells continued to explode outside. Lobo spoke. "When the pony soldiers hear no more shooting from us they will think we are beaten and move closer. This would be bad. It would give us less freedom of movement if we are forced to leave the village. But if we hold the soldiers where they now are then they would not see or hear us leave here should such a time come."

"Your thoughts show great wisdom," commented Coletto Negro. "What would you have us do my friend?"

Lobo pondered for a few seconds before replying. "I think that each time the big guns are fired, and the shells have burst among the rocks, then several warriors should go out from here and shoot towards the enemy. Then come back before the wagon guns sound again. It is not important for us to hit the soldiers or even aim at them. But as long as we continue to return their fire they will know we are not beaten. Then I do not think they will advance any further before the coming of night."

"This is good thinking," stated my father. "It is excellent strategy. Then, as soon as . . ." His words were interrupted by yet another cannonade from the American artillery. ". . . as soon as the sun falls from the sky we will prepare to abandon the village. We will leave a number of fires burning and tether a few worn out horses and ancient dogs close to the flames, so that their noisy complaints of the heat, together with the glow from the fires themselves, will make the soldiers believe we are still here. The nights are long now and by morning we will be far south. By the time the pony soldiers have discovered that we have fled the village, we will be close to the Mexican border. Once we are in Mexico the Americans cannot reach us there. It is their law."

"It is a good law," added Lobo. "it is a law I like very much." Several of the others laughed. This was a good sign. Now there was some hope where before there had been none.

The shaman, Juan Caballo, spoke up. "I will examine the omens. They will tell us if we shall succeed."

"Do not bother them," remarked Lobo cynically. "They must be having bad days just as we are for did they not forecast a great victory for us over the white-eyes?" The shaman answered not and shuffled into the shadows of the rocks; shadows now lengthening rapidly as the blood of the day's fighting was reflected in the crimson of the sun preparing to plunge behind the mountains.

For perhaps an hour the pattern of artillery bombardment from the American soldiers, followed immediately by rifle fire from our fleetest warriors, continued until it was too dark for either side to see well enough to carry the battle any further that day. Silence for a while. Then the sound of the trumpet from the pony soldiers' camp. Distant voices and laughter. The noises made by men and horses as mounts were unharnessed for the night. The clatter of metal eating utensils against metal plates.

From the centre of the council rocks my father issued his instructions in a low voice. Silently, all of us slipped away into the darkness to carry out his commands. It was a cold night and everyone was soon clad in thick, warm garments made of the skins of various animals. My own coat was of soft deer hide. All the horses to be taken with us had their muzzles clamped tight with strips of cloth bound around them. They would be able to breathe through their nostrils; but there would be no sound from their mouths to betray our actions. Pieces of hide were tied about their hooves to muffle the noises that they would otherwise have made as we led them across the rocks. Dogs were also muzzled and all babies were given favourite sweetmeats to suck.

The pack-animals were swiftly but quietly laden with those articles it was most necessary to take with us; all firearms and ammunition, food, water, blankets and extra clothing. Groups of aged or lame horses and dogs too old or crippled to make the journey south into Mexico, were bunched together at intervals throughout the camp, and tethered to stakes thrust deep into the ground, around piles of dry brushwood covered with large, heavy branches which would keep the fires burning most of the night. But these fires were not lit until the ghostly cavalcade of Indians and animals had moved far beyond the area which would be illuminated as soon as the torches were applied to the brushwood by those who had stayed behind briefly to perform this task.

As these few rejoined the main group we looked back and could see the bright yellow lances of flame stabbing into the darkness around them. We could hear the whinnying of the horses and the wimpering of the dogs left behind. They were far enough from the fires not to become frightened and panicky, but too close to allow them to settle down asleep noiselessly. To the troopers bivouacked below, things would appear as normal.

Our scouts reported that the way ahead was clear. Major Glencoe, fresh from the east and therefore new to Indian fighting, had neglected to post any advance pickets to keep a close watch on our camp. We mounted our ponies after leading them clear of the village, riding them slowly and cautiously for the first few miles, then hard and fast with the gags now removed from their jaws.

The first pale yellow evidence of approaching dawn found us less than ten miles from the Mexican border. Our mounts, their hearts almost bursting from the fury of the flight, were now moving at a more leisurely gait, heads low and tongues hanging from their lathered mouths. We looked little better. Most of us were slumped forward across the horses' necks. Some were even asleep, particularly the very young and the very old.

"Ee-yah!" The shrill warning cry from one of the warriors riding rearguard caused everyone to jerk upright in their saddles and turn as one to look behind them.There was a fast moving haze of dust coming towards us. Perhaps two miles away. Coletto Negro knew at once. We had deceived the pony soldiers, but we had not fooled their Indian scouts. The rapidly approaching dust cloud was caused by a small troop of cavalry led by their Pima, Papago and Maricopa allies. This was bad. If our band had been one only of warriors they would have outstripped the oncoming enemy with little difficulty, or perhaps set a deadly ambush further on. But we were encumbered by women, children and the elderly.

Coletto Negro filled the air with staccato commands which came like so many revolver shots. The non-combatants surged forward while the warriors converged on the rear of the column to undertake any defensive action that might become necessary. Our mounts were driven at a pace that would kill all but the hardiest. There was no emotional tie between an Apache and his pony. It was a means to an end, nothing more. He would ride it until it died and then pick another from among the spare herd.

A few minutes ago Mexico appeared so close. Now it seemed so distant. Everywhere there was a fine grey dust churned up by our horses' hooves. It filled the eyes, nose and mouth. Children were crying. Adults were coughing and rubbing their eyes. But still they pressed their mounts to even greater efforts; urged on by Coletto Negro and fear of the pursuing white-eye soldiers with their big guns and ruthless leader.

Yet, for some, the pace was harder on them than their ponies. One old man fell from his horse and was immediately trampled to a pulp by those following him. They had been too close to avoid him. He was left where he had fallen. Another old man, of perhaps seventy summers, dug his heels hard into the flanks of his mount and drew level with his chief. I could hear his words as he pointed back to the lifeless body. "Like him I will never make it to Mexico," he gasped. "I am too old." His face was strained and speech was difficult for him. "It is better to be killed by an enemy bullet than to die like that. Give me a rifle."

Coletto Negro understood and pointed to a pack-animal laden with spare guns. "Take one," he said. The old man did so and then rode off towards one of the many rocky outcrops which bordered our line of flight. There he dismounted, smacked his pony hard across the rump so that it rejoined the main herd and then concealed himself behind a huge boulder. Other old men, seeing his action, followed suit. Soon our rear was covered by perhaps a dozen such men carefully hidden behind the rocks which lined the trail we were following. The soldiers would be unaware of their presence until it was too late. The old men would sell their lives dearly to buy us time. It was high price to pay, but the commodity they were purchasing for us was beyond value. And they would die like warriors. So be it.

We were little more than a mile ahead of their place of ambush when we first heard sounds of sporadic firing. I looked back and saw that the dust cloud raised by the cavalry and their Indian scouts was slowly subsiding. This meant that they had no idea of the size of the force now attacking them and had stopped in their pursuit, at least temporarily, of the main body. Right now they were probably taking up defensive positions and formulating a plan of counterattack against their immediate adversaries.

For a time there was silence. Then the firing broke out again. But it was still sporadic so no all-out onslaught had yet been launched by the pony soldiers and their copper-coloured allies. And each minute, each second even, carried us closer to Mexico and safety. Looking back to that time I remember how much I admired those old men who accepted inevitable, sudden death in an attempt to save their people. Now I also envy them. Theirs was the manner in which warriors should leave this earth. Not to slowly rot away of old age in a lonely bed. Ah, but I deviate and I apologize.

# CHAPTER FOURTEEN

By now the sun was climbing steadily but without the fierce heat of summer. To the southwest the Guadalupe Mountains stood stark against the pale blue sky. Less than four miles away was Mexico. Then, across the still desert air, came the thin crackle of distant, concentrated rifle fire. We urged our mounts to their absolute limits. Some stumbled and fell and would never rise again. In each case the rider leaped clear, pulled another pony from the spare herd, remounted hastily and continued the flight south. But the flight had become a painfully slow crawl.

Two miles to go and the dust cloud was behind us again. This time it was approaching much faster than before. The horses causing it had been briefly rested by the delaying tactics of the old men. Now the old men were dead or dying and their blue-clad victors, together with their Indian scouts, were stretching their mounts to the utmost in an all-out attempt to stop us reaching the border. Many of the younger children were crying, more ponies were going down, killed by the pace, and there was a hard look in the eyes of the warriors riding at the rear.

Suddenly Coletto Negro was in the middle of his fighting men. "Kill your horses!" he shouted at them. "Kill your horses!" Even as he screamed at them he took his keen-edged skinning knife from his belt, leaned forward and slit his own pony's throat. Others did likewise and the ground around their dead and dying animals was stained dark red in many places. The main body of non-combatants continued their life or death race to the Mexican border which could now be seen ahead.

Coletto Negro crouched low behind the carcass of his dead mount. Looking back I could see the other warriors, perhaps twenty-five or thirty of them, in similar positions behind their own lifeless ponies. My father was gambling the lives of these men to save the rest of the band. Our line of flight from the council rocks was littered with the corpses of worn-out horses. He was obviously hoping that the rapidly approaching troopers, in their eagerness to catch us, would regard this larger bunch of dead animals as having succumbed in the same manner as the many they had already passed. The warriors were well concealed by their dead mounts. Each man had a rifle gripped tightly in his hands.

The pony soldiers galloped closer. Suddenly one of their Indian scouts split the air with a piercing scream of warning. But it was too late. As one man our warriors knelt and fired in the midst of the enemy. There was no escape for the troopers or their treacherous allies. Unable to control their frantic mounts, wild-eyed with fear, and covered with blood-streaked froth as they ignored the bits which dug cruelly into their mouths in vain attempts to stop them, the riders made easy targets for our fighting men. It was as if a huge scythe had swept through the air and cut the troopers and scouts from their saddles.

It ended as suddenly as it had started. For a while all we could see was a dense veil of white-grey dust which whirled and danced behind us and from which came a series of terrible screams. By the time the dense veil was merely a fine film we were across the border. And riding towards us, from out of the dust, on captured cavalry horses were Coletto Negro and his victorious warriors. They were leading army packmules laden with extra rifles and other plunder taken from the corpses which now littered the desert behind them. So successful had been their surprise offensive that none were dead and only three were wounded. However, even these injuries were such that they would live to tell their grandchildren how they got the scars. Stumbling along at the rear were two white-eye soldiers linked to one of the horses by lengths of rawhide.

The women and children jeered and threw rocks at these two unfortunates as they passed. For them it would have been better had they been killed in battle like their comrades. Although I had never before witnessed the Apaches torture anyone to death, I knew that this was to be the fate of these two terrified prisoners. It was the custom. Kind to their own people, the Apaches were among the most barbaric in the world when it came to torturing enemy captives. Their cruelty was inbred and knew no bounds.

Both soldiers fell to the ground in front of the chief immediately he dismounted. They begged for mercy. The tears from their eyes left small channels of a lighter colour through the grime of their faces. But their pleas were as husks of corn hurled into an approaching wind, for they never reached my father's ears. He looked at them with scorn and hatred in his eyes. "Tie them together while we eat!" he ordered. "Then we will take them with us to a place beyond the range of the big guns of the pony soldier chief, for he will not cross the border."

Even as the struggling captives were being bound back to back by a handful of warriors, the rest were gorging themselves on the raw meat of a freshly-killed horse. There would be no time to cook food in this place and we needed nourishment to replace the energy consumed by the long miles behind us. Soon the women and children too were eating raw flesh torn from the dead horse.

Another was killed. The blood was given to the babies to drink. My own stomach was tight with hunger. I tentatively placed a small piece of raw horseflesh in my mouth and started chewing. It was sweet and sickly, but I was as weak as the rest because of the emptiness inside so I ate until the hunger was appeased. Although, I must confess, to this day I have never cultivated a taste for raw meat. It is simply that what one must do to stay alive, one does.

Coletto Negro allowed us the maximum rest period possible; and that was until the lookouts he had posted reported seeing Major Glencoe's main force in the distance. Immediately the command was spotted by these scouts we were soon packed and on the move again. The two captured troopers were placed on separate mounts, with their wrists bound behind their backs and their two ponies linked together with a single strip of rawhide. One, tall and blonde-haired, could not have been more than eighteen or nineteen years old. He was whimpering. The other, not as tall, bald and thickset, was perhaps twice the age of the young one. He tried to show no fear. But it was there in his eyes. He could not hide it completely.

For the first time in many days we were light at heart. We rode much slower and with ease. Coarse jests concerning the many varied ways of prolonging the agonizing deaths of the two prisoners were thrown back and forth.

Several miles from the border I looked back. It was exactly as Coletto Negro had stated. The massive dust cloud was returning north. Major Glencoe had not crossed into Mexico. But we continued riding until our chief ordered us to halt. He did so at a place where the rocky ground over which we had been travelling suddenly surrendered to an area of soft white sand. Its only feature was a dead tree which thrust itself upwards from the desert like a gaunt white skeleton rising from the grave. Denuded of its bark long ago by the merciless sun and driving sandstorms, even its two remaining branches reached outwards like human arms stripped of all their flesh.

Coletto Negro turned to those men closest to him. "Here they will die," he said simply. His voice was without emotion, but hatred showed clearly in his eyes. We all dismounted and the women began making camp. One of the braves slaughtered an army pack-mule which some of the women immediately started skinning and butchering. Cooked mule meat was a great delicacy among the Apaches.

At the same time the feast was being prepared so was the torture of the two captive troopers. The warrior supervising the task was short even by Apache standards. His extemely bowed legs caused him to waddle rather than walk, he had a childhood injury to his mouth which made his speech so incoherent that it sounded like a turkey's gobble and he was unbelievably ugly. He was aptly named. Zopilote — turkey buzzard. All Apaches enjoyed killing their enemies but this one derived so much satisfaction from it that he had turned it into a macabre art.

He ordered one prisoner suspended from a limb of the dead tree by his ankles, so that his head was about two or three feet above the ground. The other was buried up to his neck in the soft sand. Only his head was visible. Both were positioned so that each faced the other. The perspiration rolled down their foreheads, at first like ever-increasing cascades of glass beads and then in continuous rivulets. But it was not the sweat which comes to a man when he is hot, but that of absolute fear.

Zopilote drew his skinning knife from the top of one of his moccasins. The blade was honed to the sharpness of a razor's edge. Slowly he approached the pony-soldier buried in the sand. This was the young one with hair the colour of ripened corn. The youth screamed and rolled his head from side to side. The excitement which this aroused in Zopilote caused him to sound more like the bird of carrion after which he had been named. But he was in no hurry. He stopped short of his victim and squatted on his haunches. What was intended to be a smile forced his deformed mouth into a ugly leer. He was enjoying the moment, savouring it like a man does a good brandy. Perhaps such times helped ease the inner torments created by his grotesque appearance. I do not know.

The young soldier continued to move his head frantically in all directions. The tears ran down his face and were quickly devoured by the dry white sand. ''Oh my God!'' he sobbed. ''Oh my God!'' His voice reached a crescendo. ''For Christ's sake let me outa here!'' he shrieked.

''Take it easy son.'' The words came from his battle-seasoned colleague hanging face downwards in front of him. ''The more you carry on, the longer it'll take. We're gonna die so let's get it over with as quickly as possible.'' Zopilote turned round on his haunches and struck the soldier across the mouth. He started to swing gently from the limb to which his ankles were bound with rawhide, and blood trickled slowly from his lips. He spat in Zopilote's face. This spurred the ugly Apache into action and he swiftly built a small fire beneath the swaying figure above him.

I realized afterwards that this was why the pony soldier with little hair had spat at Zopilote. Whatever was going to happen would be agonizing, but this way it would be quicker. As the tiny flames reached lazily upwards and began to singe away the hair that ringed his otherwise bald head, the old trooper bit deeply into his lips to hold back the cries which would come soon enough.

But by now the young one was screaming wildly. He closed his eyes to the horrifying sight immediately in front of him. Zopilote saw this and cut away the boy's eyelids with two deft strokes of the skinning knife. Now he would have to watch the terrifying ordeal of the older man who had started screaming immediately the heat of the fire began to stretch the skin across his head like an ancient yellow parchment.

At this point the remainder of the band, women and children included, had stopped whatever they had been doing and were clustered around the pain-wracked soldiers. Zopilote grunted in satisfaction. He had an audience and was making the most of it. For a man like himself such occasions were rare. At other times few wished to look at him, particularly the women. He had never had a women of his own. Only the ones taken occasionally from other Indian tribes, Mexican villages or American wagon trains and ranch houses. But they never lasted long. His heart was as ugly as his face.

Now the skin covering the old man's head burst and peeled back slowly leaving the white bones of his skull exposed to the heat of the flames below. "Bastards! Bastards! Bastards!" he yelled as the pain became unbearable. His young friend had fainted. Zopilote noticed this and cuffed him back to consciousness with the palm and rear of his left hand. The skinning knife was still clasped in his right hand. With the point of it he nicked the corners of the boy's eyes, ears, nostrils and mouth so that the blood ran slowly down his face onto the area around his head.

They came from nowhere. The vicious ants of the desert. Where previously there had been nothing but grains of white sand there was now a steady stream of these minute but deadly creatures. Following the tiny trails of blood, they ate into the screaming youth's mouth, nose, eyes and ears. They would not stop until they had cleaned every last vestige of flesh from his bones. Soon his mouth was so filled with ants that he could no longer scream. But he was still alive. The exposed eyeballs rolled in terror. The head moved feebly in agony. He would die slowly.

A few feet ahead of him the skull of the other pony soldier suddenly cracked open like a ripe pinon seed and his brains spattered onto the fire beneath. I slid quickly away and crouched low behind a pile of plunder. Immediately I was hidden from the others I vomited and vomited until it felt as if my stomach was trying to force its way upwards through my mouth. But as soon as the feeling of nausea had abated sufficiently, I kicked sand over the area around me to conceal all traces of what any true Apache would consider a weakness. Then I quickly rejoined the band. No one had missed me and I kept well to the rear so that I saw no more of the horrifying spectacle which the rest so obviously were enjoying.

You are shocked by what I tell you senor. Yet have I not already stated that the Apaches were among the most barbaric peoples of the world and that their cruelty knew no bounds? They were savages living in a savage land. They knew no other way. But theirs was an honest cruelty if I may be permitted to say such a thing. They did not hide it beneath the polished surface of civilization and pretend that it did not exist.

You look puzzled. Let me give you an example of what I am trying to explain. In 1913, nearly fifty years after the torture of those two soldiers, the dictator of Mexico, General Victoriano Huerta, was attempting to subdue a revolutionary movement led by Emiliano Zapata, Alvaro Obregon and Pancho Villa. In his anger and frustration at being completely outmanoeuvred by these men on so many occasions, he turned his Federal Militia, the Rurales, against everyone of whom he was even slightly suspicious. Whether they were guilty or not was of no consequence to him. I once watched his officers have their men bury fellow Mexicans, Huerta's own people, many of them loyal to him until that moment, up to their necks in the ground. And then gallop their horses across these unfortuantes until their skulls cracked like so many eggshells. That is what I mean by cruelty concealed by the polished surface we call civilization.

In many parts of the world similar situations exist even today under the guise of our so-called civilized society. Now do you understand what I mean when I refer to Apache cruelty as ''honest?'' They did not know that what they were doing was wrong. Civilization knows such actions are wrong and yet it often condones them. I am not defending Apache barbarism. What they did was very wrong. It is simply that I am attempting to place before you a picture of the way things were and why they were that way. Now you understand? That is good.

# CHAPTER FIFTEEN

Early summer 1868. We had been in Mexico almost three years and I was now fifteen years old. The age when a youth became an apprentice warrior. Our camp, deep in the Sierra Madre mountains of northern Sonora, was a short distance from the source of the Rio Yaqui and less than fifty miles from the Arizona border. The band was still a compact unit under Coletto Negro and our fighting men regularly made forays into many parts of Sonora and Arizona. Sometimes they even undertook longer raids into the adjoining Mexican state of Chihuahua or north of the border into New Mexico. Once again these were good times for us. And for me especially. This summer I was to go on my first raid.

Here I was in the country of my birth; and yet I had no desire at all to return to my own people. I had grown to love the wild free life of the Apache. Cabeza had already served his apprenticeship and was now a young warrior. How I envied him. He sat proud and tall astride his war pony and only his blue eyes betrayed the fact that he had been born white. I think he was as eager as I was for me to become a fully fledged fighting man, so that our friendship could once again become as firm as it had been when we were younger. For warriors had comrades only among other warriors. That was how it was with the Apache fighting elite.

I had been well prepared for this first raid for which I had volunteered. My father was a good teacher. In order to become a recognized fighter I knew that I would have to volunteer for four such war parties. And tomorrow was to see the first of them.

As soon as the intended raid had been announced I had immediately requested permission to take part. Having already been out with many hunting parties and shown my abilities at tracking, stalking and using the bow and arrow, I now felt I was ready for my first war party. Permission had been granted and I had at once felt several inches taller.

That night a special ceremony was held in my honour, during which I was presented with a shield and helmet as was the custom. Then the war dance began. It was an eerie but exciting event staged against a back-drop of darkness illuminated only by the prancing flames of a huge fire. I knew what was expected of me. All eyes would be on me during the dance, watching my endurance and agility. I spurted forwards, leaped high into the air and twisted my body in all directions in a non-stop marathon of these repetitious movements which seemed to last all night. The sweat brought on by this frantic display of energy, the heat of the night and the fire around which we were dancing, ran down my body in rivulets. It soaked my hair and clouded my eyes. I felt completely exhausted but it now felt as if someone else had entered my body and refused to stop the apparently endless stamping and jerking. Then, as abruptly as it had started so the pounding of war drums ceased. I staggered lifelessly away from the heat of the dying fire and into the welcome darkness which was no longer oppressively hot but refreshingly cool. As I did so I looked back. The sight of several seasoned warriors slumped wearily on the ground around the fire lifted some of the tiredness from my body, but not sufficient to keep me from sleeping immediately I entered my father's wickiup. Even the exciting thoughts of my first raid on the morrow, which had filled my head for so many days and nights, failed to keep me awake on this occasion.

The camp was already alive with the boisterous activity that always preceded a raid when I finally stirred. I do not believe that there was a single muscle in my entire body which did not ache. I groaned as I slowly raised myself from the hard floor on which I had fallen asleep before reaching the buffalo robes and Navajo blankets which were my bed. My father looked in and grinned. "So you are still alive? When I passed you a short while ago I had serious doubts as to what I should do. Whether to send for the medicine man or a burial party. But, I decided to wait awhile before making any decision. And now I see that you are recovered. Unfortunately for you my son, however, we have already eaten and are almost ready to start. So you must make your preparations rapidly and eat later. Unless, of course, you no longer wish to join us." So saying, he turned and strode from the wickiup.

Despite the pains that stabbed at my every part I leaped after him, stopping only to snatch up my bow and quiver of arrows. Outside, the sun was a huge white disc of fire low on the horizon but climbing steadily. The heat waves it created were rising from the rocks all around and were giving everything in sight an illusion of tremulous motion. I raced across the ground to my tethered pony, a beautiful light brown animal presented to me by Lobo immediately after I had been given permission to join the war party. Within minutes I had him ready. Then I sped on foot to where the main body was grouped and making final preparations.

An apprentice did not fight during the four raids of his novitiate. His sole task was to help the warriors in every other way possible, and to perform all the menial duties. He had to care for the ponies, build fires and keep them burning, cook meals, stand guard at night and constantly tend to all the needs of the warriors.

Such chores were not for them. Their business was fighting and plundering and nothing else.

Although the war party was almost ready, I was still able to help load the pack animals with food, water and additional ammunition and firearms. The traditional weapons of the Apache were a lance, about fiteen feet in length, and a powerful bow with arrows of rush or cane. These last were more than three feet long and tipped with iron, bone or stone. Many warriors were able to kill at a distance of five hundred feet with the bow and arrow. But in the majority of cases, these primitive weapons had been replaced by the white man's rifle with which the Apache was no less skilled.

The village we attacked was a day's ride southwest from our camp. However, I cannot recall its name because it no longer exists other than in the memories of any surviving inhabitants, for all fled their homes following this raid. They had been plundered by the Apaches many times before and had still remained. But this time it was different. The federal soldiers were waiting for us. I learned many years later that they had been on the trail of a gang of bandits which had rested briefly during its flight to sample, against the villagers' wishes, their women, liquor and food.

The troopers, no better than the bandits, had likewise stopped for a while to try the delights of the village, once again contrary to the desires of the people, before continuing the chase. Seeing our dust in the distance the militia had mistaken us for the bandits. Thinking they were returning for further spoils the soldiers had set a trap.

Anticipating no opposition, we followed our customary practice of entering the village like a solitary pack of wolves. Apaches were hated as much by the army as were the bandits so we rode into a terrible crossfire from all sides. Several of our best fighting men were left dead or dying in the small plaza. Fortunately, however the over-eager militia opened fire too soon for the ambush to be wholly successful and most of us were able to wheel our mounts around and escape the ambuscade.

But when the federal troopers left the village the following morning so did its entire population. Not to chase bandits, as was the case with the militia, but to escape the Apache retribution which they considered inevitable.

And so it was. Not for them, however, but for the troopers. Immediately after our flight from the Mexican soldiers' bullets we had ridden hard for some rocky terrain perhaps two or three miles northwest of the village. There a count had revealed that eleven of the original war party of seventy warriors had been cut down by the militia. Angry and bitter, Coletto Negro had sent two scouts to watch the village while the rest us had waited patiently all night. Now it was well into the morning. Obviously the soldiers were not early risers. They had probably been sleeping off a night of debauchery following their victory.

An hour or so before noon our scouts were seen approaching at a fast gallop. One of them was Cabeza. Sliding quickly sideways from his panting and lathered mount he ran across to my father. "Everyone is leaving the village," he gasped,.

"Everyone?" echoed Coletto Negro in amazement.

"Yes my chief," replied Cabeza. "The peons have laden all their possessions onto mules and even handcarts. They are obviously very frightened that we will return now the soldiers are leaving."

"In which direction do they go?" demanded Coletto Negro.

"Southwest towards the bigger towns where there will be more protection for them and their families."

"Not the villagers. The soldiers. Where are they headed?"

"Almost due north. They are following the tracks of a number of horses. They will pass by us perhaps four miles east of here. There are but forty men in the patrol."

For a while the chief was silent. When he finally spoke he smiled. But it was not a pleasant smile. "They are going in the general direction of Canyon del Muerte." This was a box canyon, with but one way in and no other way out, situated approximately fifteen miles north of the village. "It is there that we shall meet and talk with them. But this time it will be Apaches' bullets which do the speaking."

"Perhaps they do not ride that way," ventured Lobo.

The chief smiled again. "You, my good friend, together with nine others, will ensure that they do. You will ride ahead of them. Follow the same tracks which they follow. But do not let them see you. At the place where the trail left by the men they seek leads away from the Canyon del Muerte erase all traces of it. Then make your own tracks lead clearly to the canyon. We will wait for you. And then, together, we will wait for the soldiers. Pick your men and go now."

Lobo rapidly chose his nine riders. I was one of them and felt so proud. We rode relentlessly until we reached the trail the Mexican militia was following. Leisurely pursuers, even at their very best, the troopers were not in sight yet. Lobo led us all onto the well-trodden trail and told us to dismount. While two held the horses, the rest of us, upon his instructions, oblitered, with the aid of brushwood and blankets, all evidence of our link-up with the path ridden by the men being chased by the Mexican patrol.

Keeping well ahead of the soldiers, we galloped our ponies hard along the path until a short distance from the canyon, it veered to the northeast. Here we dismounted again. But this time it was to eradicate the tracks where they branched away from the route we wished the patrol to take. Remounting hastily, we rode swiftly to the Canyon del Muerte. Whoever the soldiers were following would now appear to have gone straight into the canyon.

When we rejoined Coletto Negro he was already preparing his ambush. The canyon was a natural amphitheatre, encircled by terraces of irregular rocky platforms that stretched upwards for perhaps two hundred feet. Knowing that even the dimwitted Mexicans would realize they were heading into an ambush, the chief set his trap accordingly.

Together with three youths who had not yet completed their novitiate, I was ordered into a small arroyo at the end of the canyon. The entrance was well concealed by boulders, and it was behind these that the four of us were to hold the horses.

Coletto Negro then divided his force into two. I watched as twelve warriors strung themselves out behind the many rocks that littered the lowest terrace of this huge red amphitheatre which was being prepared for a Mexican tragedy. These same warriors deliberately left the muzzles of their weapons protruding from among the rocks so that the bright sun glinted from a dozen rifle barrels. Anticipating that the soldiers would see these, and move in along the natural platform immediately above, in order to fire down on their would-be ambushers, he planted the remainder of his warriors even higher up the face of the canyon.

Some time elapsed before we saw the expected dust cloud approaching the entrance to the Canyon del Muerte. Slowly, it subsided. Silently, on foot, the troopers filed through the entrance at a level above the twelve warriors with whom Coletto Negro baited his trap. Once all forty were in position, the officer in charge raised his sword. His men stood up, placed their rifles to their shoulders and aimed at the figures below. Whether the soldiers were surprised when they discovered their quarry was a band of Apaches instead of a gang of bandits I shall never know, for Coletto Negro had planned his ambush to perfection.

Before the officer could lower his sword in silent signal for firing to commence, he and many of his men were cut down by a deadly raid of bullets which poured from the guns of the Apaches stationed above them. The Mexicans turned to meet this new, unexpected menace; and were at once caught in a ruthless crossfire from above and below. Many threw down their weapons and cried out for mercy. One screamed: "Madre de Dios! Madre de . . ." Blood, gushing from an ugly hole which suddenly appeared in his throat, cut off any further words. Mercy was not part of the Apache vocabulary.

As soon as the final semblance of Mexican resistance ended, so did the firing of the warriors. Then, as one, they scrambled from all directions across the rock face towards the defeated soldiers. Any who were still breathing were pounded to death with rocks. Then the Apaches literally hacked the corpses to pieces with their sharp knives. A dismembered enemy was no enemy at all should he ever be encountered again in the spirit world.

As Coletto Negro and his triumphant fighting men strode towards us and their horses I could see that no one was missing or even injured. The entire ambuscade had lasted less time than it takes a good runner to cover two miles. They were all staggering under the weight of weapons, ammunition and other items stripped from the soldiers' bodies. And, beyond the mouth of the Canyon del Muerte, in English this means canyon of death, were waiting the forty horses of the dead Mexicans. Our war leader had turned a bad raid into a good one.

But the eleven dead warriors lay heavy in our hearts. Despite the rich plunder we had gained it was too high a price to pay. Before returning to our camp we rode back to the Mexican village to loot it and bury those killed by the militia. There was little left to bury, however, for their corpses had been piled into a grotesque heap in the centre of the plaza and burned. It was a grisly sight and I was glad that the soldiers had suffered and died back there in the canyon.

# CHAPTER SIXTEEN

The summer passed slowly with its apparently endless heat searing everything to a brittle hardness. Only in the mountains was there any coolness. On the lower levels the relentless sun scorched all it touched. Even the people of this land were dark and wrinkled like over-dried prunes. The creases that lined the faces of these Mexican peons, however, were not put there by the heat alone or by old age. But also by ceaseless toil and worry. Their crops could be grown only with the aid of irrigation and continual back-breaking labour. Then, when the crops were finally harvested, the majority would go in taxes or be taken by bandits or Apaches.

If the peons were fortunate, then just sufficient would be left to feed them through the winter; so that the entire wearying process could commence again the following year. For neither bandits nor Apaches would normally be foolish enough to kill off a source of supply. And yet these peasants never seemed to question the futility of their existence. Or was it futile? Who can say? For in any final analysis the farmers always remained even if many of their numbers died. But those who plundered eventually succumbed, as law and order slowly, yet remorselessly, moved in to protect those who worked the land. If I ever envied the patience and fortitude of those peasant farmers, or perhaps they were merely fatalists, I never once envied the lives they led.

The second and third raids of my novitiate passed without any further deaths, or even injuries among the fighting men, for we had learned well from the lesson earlier that summer. Never again did we ride into a village in a single group but, instead, would strike it from all sides after having first scouted it thoroughly.

Now we were preparing for the final raid of the year. Summer had gradually surrendered to autumn which would, in turn, inevitably give way to winter. Winter in the mountains was always ruthlessly cold and only the hardiest ventured far from the warmth of their lodges. But even they remained immobile when the great snows came. So that last raid of any year was always the biggest and the most thorough. It had to be for much food, additional clothing and blankets were needed to withstand the ravages of winter. For me there was an added significance. This war party, my fourth, would see the end of my apprenticeship. After this I would be a warrior and no longer a holder of horses or lighter of fires.

The village we were to attack was a large one. Too large I thought. But the summer had been far hotter and drier than normal, and the harvested crops were of poor quality. The war council, therefore, had argued that only a big village or small town would contain sufficient food and other necessities to supply the hugh quantities of provision we would require to keep us healthy until the following spring.

For a day we travelled southeast until we linked up with the Rio de Bavispe where we camped until dawn. The sun, partially obscured above and below by layers of red-tinted clouds, slowly peered over the distant horizon like a bleary, half-open, bloodshot eye. There was a chill in the air which seemed to probe every part of my body and my teeth were chattering. Even before the other apprentice warriors were fully awake, I was busily building a cooking fire. Not that I was over-anxious to do this particular chore, but the activity started my blood circulating freely and a warm glow invaded those areas which had previously been shivering with the cold of the early morning. A hastily devoured breakfast and we were once again astride our horses. This time riding due south, following the river as it rippled, drifted, gurgled and swirled its way towards the far-off ocean.

That day we covered perhaps seventy-five or eighty miles before we stopped. It was dark and very late. As I helped the other apprentices prepare the evening meal Coletto Negro called together a council of his best fighting men. The dancing flames of the fire we had just lit fashioned and erased, in rapid succession, countless weird patterns on their copper-coloured bodies. The flickering glow gave an eerie aspect to their faces. I saw my father jab a finger towards the southwest and speak rapidly to the cream of his warriors gathered around him.

Unable to hear what they were saying, I decided to look in the direction in which he had pointed. Two or three miles away, on the other side of the river, were literally hundreds of lights. Some went out as the occupants of those buildings retired for the night. Others came on, probably as those who lived there drifted home after an evening's drinking at one or more of the local cantinas. The number of lights produced a coldness in my stomach. There was no doubt in my mind. This was not merely a large village as had been stated prior to sending out the war party. It was not a small town either. It was at the very least a fair-sized town, with probably seven or eight hundred men capable of bearing arms. We had little more than one hundred warriors. If I slept at all that night then it was very uneasy and fitful sleep.

It was still dark when a hand grabbed my shoulder and shook me roughly. All around me figures were stirring and moving about quietly. As I rushed to gather brushwood to build a fire Coletto Negro hissed: "No fires! There is no time for cooking. We will eat as we ride. We must have the town surrounded before the sun comes up." With these few terse words he strode over to his horse and mounted. Soon we were all jogging gently through the darkness, chewing on strips of dried meat as the sturdy war ponies moved steadily forward. The air was raw and there was a numbness in my bones.

After perhaps a mile, the leading warriors started crossing the river at a very shallow point. Awaiting us on the opposite bank was a small cluster of barely discernible figures on horseback. They were scouts sent out during the night to investigate every entrance into the town, so that we could hit it from as many sides as possible immediately the sun cast its first pale light across the sky.

Urgent whispers back and forth between the scouts and the war leaders, indicated an anxiety concerning the size of the town. But Coletto Negro, supported firmly by Lobo and another leading warrior, Lince, argued that we had two distinct advantages over the sleeping Mexicans; speed and surprise. Besides, where else would we get sufficient provsions to maintain our entire band during the approaching cold season other than in a community of a similar size to the one now stretched before us? It was much too late for a series of raids against small, isolated villages scattered across many hundreds of miles.

Lobo lived up to his name which, in English, means wolf. "Are we warriors or women?" he snarled. There was immediate silence. This was a terrible insult to any fighting men and an open challenge.

Spitting like the bobcat after which he had been named, the small, wiry Lince sided with him. "You heard the words of Lobo," he hissed. "Are we warriors or women?"

Faced with such an ultimatum, any man who backed down from the fight ahead would be branded a coward. No one was ever forced to join a war party. The choice lay always with the individual for the Apache society was a truly democratic one. But to abandon a raid after he had committed himself would bring a warrior absolute rejection, contempt and ridicule from his fellow braves, until he either left the band or redeemed himself in their eyes.

No one backed down.

Silently we approached the outskirts of the town, where small groups of warriors broke away from the main body and, wraith-like, disappeared into the darkness. Soon they would all be in prearranged positions awaiting their chief's wolf howl signal to launch the attack. Together with the other apprentices and the remuda of spare horses, I remained a hundred or so yards north of the town. It would be our task to aid any injured warriors after the raid, and to help load and manage the pack animals. I shivered as I waited. But this time it was not because of the cold.

Even before the sun itself appeared in the sky, its wan light slowly silhouetted the sprawling mass of angular, flat-roofed, single-story adobe structures that littered the landscape immediately ahead. Never before had I seen such a large community.

The eerie wail of a wolf shattered the still morning air. A short silence, then two more howls. This was the signal. It was as if the town was suddenly engulfed by an immense tidal wave of brown bodies and horses of all colours. The faces of the screaming warriors were streaked with vermilion. Sleepy-eyed Mexicans stumbled in amazement from their doorways and were immediately hacked or shot down.

But there were wiser heads among them. Perhaps they had experienced Indian attacks before. Many of them were armed. They barricaded their doors and returned the fire of the Apaches. Most of their guns spoke with old voices. Yet even an ancient firearm is a deadly thing when gripped in steady hands. And so it was that some of our warriors fell from their mounts never to ride again.

One brave came galloping towards us leading a fully laden pack-mule. He jerked his horse to a standstill and handed the reins of the pack animal to one of the apprentices. "Here, small one, take these," he gapsed. "I will be back again very soon." But as he wheeled his mount around I saw the ugly red hole in his back. A few yards short of the town he tumbled from his horse.

I vaulted astride my pony and dug my heels into its flanks. It responded like an arrow from a bow and sped towards the fallen warrior. The other apprentices shouted after me but, I reasoned with myself, was not helping the wounded one of our main duties? As soon as I reached him I slid to the ground. He turned to face me and tried to speak. But the words became incoherent as blood dribbled from between his lips. A few seconds later he was dead. I tried to lift his body onto his mount which stood close by with lathered jaws and heaving sides. It was impossible, however, for he was far too heavy.

Grabbing his rifle and the reins of his horse I remounted my own pony and turned to rejoin the other trainee warriors. But, glancing back briefly towards the town, I saw a Mexican standing a few yards away in the doorway of an adobe building. The stock of his rifle was braced firmly into his right shoulder. Its barrel was following the progress of a swiftly approaching Apache who was completely unaware of what awaited him.

Never before had I fired a gun but I had seen it done many times. In the midst of the noisy confusion and swirling dust of the attack the Mexican had not noticed me. I slid from my pony, rested the dead warrior's rifle across its back, aimed and fired. My ears were suddenly filled with the sound of thunder, my lungs were filled with smoke and my eyeballs felt as if they were on fire. Yet none of these things mattered as, through my blurred vision, I saw the Mexican drop his weapon and stagger into the open. His hands clutched at his stomach as if trying to tear out the bullet embedded there.

"Many thanks young warrior," calmly came a voice from beside me. My heart leaped. The man I had saved was Lobo and he had called me 'young warrior'.

I swiftly jumped astride my pony, rifle in hand, and turned to join the battle. A strong yet gentle hand upon my shoulder restrained me. "You have done sufficient for one day," said Lobo quietly. "Now rejoin your friends. We will have need of you soon for the fight goes our way and there will be many packhorses for you to handle before long." And then he was gone. Back into the noise, dust and smoke from which would come our winter provisions.

Fourteen braves died that morning. When we returned to our camp in the Sierra Madre mountains two days later, there was much wailing and grief among the women. Many had lost husbands, sons, fathers and brothers. For them there was little immediate compensation other than the fact that their men had not died for nothing. There was now enough food, clothing and blankets to see the remainder of us through the long cold months ahead. And there were several young captive Mexican boys who would later be distributed among the families to be raised as Apache fighting men just as I had been.

The raid ended for me in the climax of intense personal pride when Lobo presented me with a beautifully engraved Mexican rifle, before the entire band, for saving his life. That winter I went on hunting expeditions whenever the weather permitted and became a reasonable shot with the weapon.

During the years that followed, life became as good for us in old Mexico as it had been in New Mexico before the American soldiers forced us to flee south. Cabeza and I developed an even deeper comradeship than the one which had existed between us during those days preceding our warrior status. We went on many raids together. Yet, looking back, I remember none of them so vividly as the one which ended my novitiate and saw me become a true fighting member of the Apache nation.

# CHAPTER SEVENTEEN

She rode into our camp in the summer of 1873, together with her father, mother and two younger brothers. They had fled the barren San Carlos reservation in Arizona where the Apaches were dying from American ill-treatment in general and disease and a shortage of food in particular. They wanted to join our band. Coletto Negro welcomed them.

She was darker skinned than any other other Apache I had ever seen. And her face was not as rounded as those of most Apache women. Her features were delicate yet not without strength. She carried herself with a graceful dignity. I felt that the blood of an ancient, long-forgotten Aztec dynasty was probably strong within her.

Her lips were not the thin lips of the Apache. But full and always smiling. She was called Sagozhuni which, in the Apache tongue, means "pretty mouth." I was in my twentieth year and she had only fifteen summers behind her. Yet, even though she was not ready for marriage, a strange sensation deep within my stomach told me that she would be my woman when the time was right.

Before she could become eligible for marriage, however, Sagozhuni would have to go through the traditonal Apache ceremony that would take her from puberty to womanhood. This was another reason for leaving the San Carlos reservation. Sagozhuni was ready to become a woman but her mother had not wanted the cermony to take place before the mocking eyes of the Americans.

Neither had the girl's father, for he had noticed several of the soldiers stationed nearby looking covetously at his daughter. He had no desire for them to use her. He wanted her to marry an Apache warrior. And he wanted his two young sons to know the freedom he had experienced as a youth, and to grow into fighting men just as he had. So, with all these things in mind, he had slipped quietly away from the reservation with his family one night and travelled south to our camp in Mexico.

The family's celebration of Sagozhuni's puberty had already taken place before she had joined us. As with all Apaches it had been a simple affair, during which she would have been told to run towards the east, the point from which the sun rises, as an indication that she had reached womanhood.

A month or two following the family celebration would come the real ceremony in which the whole band would participate.

Sagozhuni's coming-out party, as it would be called today, took place after her family had been with us little more than a month. During this period I had seen her only occasionally, for hunting and raiding parties were once again being sent out regularly, and I spent little time in the village.

Her family had arrived with scant provisions and even fewer personal possessions. The cost of the ceremony would be high. But the men and women of our village called upon the family frequently and always left a variety of gifts before departing. This was the Apache way. By the time of the festival, which would last four days, the family had sufficient supplies to feed all those who would attend. The women of the band constructed the animal-skin tepee which would be the girl's home for the four days and nights of the ceremony. They also helped make the beautifully decorated costume which she would wear during those same days and nights.

Then came the day. No more hunting or war parties would be sent out during the ceremony. Nobody in the band wanted to miss the festival. And no one did. It was the biggest and, because of Sagozhuni, the most beautiful I ever witnessed during my time with the Apaches.

The girl's father, called Jayan, the strong one, was content to have our medicine man conduct the religious rites of the ceremony. The shaman's name was Aguila. In English this means the eagle. He was well-called, for he saw everything and was held in great respect; unlike his predecessor, Juan Caballo, who had been ridiculed openly by Lobo during the fight with Major Glencoe's pony soldiers.

Ah, senor, it is as yesterday. The sky was a great splash of vivid blue, the sun was all-powerful and the still air was filled with the music of the many song-birds which nested among the great variety of trees ringing our mountain camp. It was one of the hottest days I had known. Too hot. Together with my good friend, Cabeza, I lay sprawled on my stomach in the shadow of a ledge which jutted out from a rock face bordering the village. Although we were both lying down, the ground climbed steadily at this point and we were able to see clearly Sagozhuni's tepee and all that occurred in the immediate vicinity of her ritual home.

As the hour drew closer, a file of women entered the tepee carrying food and gifts. After the last of them had emerged once again into the open, so Sagozhuni made her appearance. She was clothed in her finest array. Her dress and moccasins were of white buckskin adorned with multi-coloured beads, bright metal ornaments and a variety of amulets.

But if her apparel was attractive to behold, her own physical beauty was completely breath-taking. Her long jet-black hair was drawn back to the nape of her neck so that no line of her features was hidden. There was loveliness in every aspect of her deep brown face. The full lips, still smiling, and the white teeth they disclosed, were like a solitary ray of dazzling sunshine penetrating an otherwise dark sky. Her buckskin dress had been so softened that it clearly displayed the pointed outlines of her small, firm breasts. As she walked, with unhurried dignity and an easy grace, towards the tepee, the lines of her flat stomach and slim thighs also became visible.

Suddenly an elbow was thrust roughly into my ribs. I turned. "Why is it that I waste so much breath on you?" sighed Cabeza. "I speak and yet you do not hear a single word."

I felt embarrassed but tried to appear otherwise. "I am sorry my friend," I replied. "It is the sun. The heat made me sleepy."

"Since when did a man sleep with his eyeballs protruding from their sockets?"

I ignored the question and covered up by countering with one of my own. "What was it then that you were saying as I dozed in the sun?" I asked.

"It does not matter. Whatever I was saying is clearly reflected in your eyes which sleep while they are still wide open."

"I do not understand," I said in confusion, for I knew only too well what he meant.

"All right my friend. Then I will repeat that which I have already stated, although I am convinced that your ignorance is an absolute pretence. I said that she is very beautiful is she not?"

"Who? Oh, Sagozhuni. Er . . . yes, she is quite pretty."

"Quite pretty? Now I know that you lie Cuchillo, for on every occasion you have seen her since the day she arrived you have had eyes for nothing else. Do you consider me a fool?"

"That I would never do my friend for does not Cabeza mean the clever one?" I sighed. "You are right. She is very beautiful and she stirs me inside a great deal more than I would wish."

"Nonsense. It is good for a man to be stirred by a woman. Without such stirrings you and I would not be here and the earth would soon be without people."

"But she is so young," I protested.

Cabeza's face took on a solemn look. "In four days she will be a woman. And there are other young braves as eager to possess her as you are. Yet they will not think her too young. I have seen it in their eyes while you have been looking only at her."

"This is true?"

"It is true," replied Cabeza. "So from our next raids you must bring back many horses and gifts for her parents. I will help you. And, remember, in her father's eyes you have one great advantage over all your rivals. You are the chief's son."

"You are a good friend," I said simply and, with this thing settled in our minds, we turned as one to see Sagozhuni bend low to enter her tepee. She was followed by her attendants.

Her four days and nights inside the tepee would be spent in long hours of statuesque kneeling alternated with strenuous yet stately ceremonial dances. The crowd outside had already commenced dancing and feasting. Throughout the second day the social activities of the band continued around the tepee. Inside, Sagozhuni carried on her exhausting dancing and supplications.

Some of the women had brewed an immense quantity of tiswin, the Indians' answer to the white man's beer. It was not a very potent drink, however, and never caused drunkenness; unless taken in large amounts following periods of prolonged fasting. As it was, the women had made sure that their men had eaten before, and while, they were drinking the tiswin. For a drunken warrior was usually a very dangerous man, and they did not want Sagozhuni's puberty ritual marred in any manner. But, if none of the men were actually drunk, they were certainly somewhat unsteady in their movements as a result of their frequent visits to the huge container of native beer.

On the third night the devil dancers appeared and cavorted wildly around a central fire. The flames seemed to dance with them and caused their bodies, disguised by skins taken from a variety of wild animals, to present an even more savage and frightening aspect. Initially, the other members of the village pretended to be afraid of these fierce creatures but, after failing to drive them off, joined them in their wild and exhilarating dancing.

For a period Sagozhuni came out from her tent of animal hides and also danced with them. I quietly left the circle of sweating, half-drunken figures leaping around the fire so that I could watch her from the darkness beyond the area illuminated by the flames. She looked very weary and her movements were no longer graceful or nimbled. Her feet dragged in the dust and once or twice she stumbled. But the smile was still there on her full lips, and her flawless teeth appeared even whiter as the light from the fire touched upon them briefly from time to time.

With the fourth and final night came the climax of the ceremony. Once again the feasting, drinking and dancing continued outside Sagozhuni's tepee while she maintained her vigils and ritual dances within the pointed structure of wooden poles covered by animal skins. As the first rays of the morning sun spread their pale light across the land, the shaman, Aguila, completed his ritualistic exercises and strode over to the tepee. Sagozhuni emerged into the open and ran through the people around her and towards the east for a short distance. During this brief time her ritual home was swiftly demolished. Then, slowly, she turned to face us. She was now a woman.

That summer I went with every war party sent from the village. And always riding beside me was Cabeza.

When the last raid of the year was over, and many of the trees that covered the mountain slopes surrounding the camps were exchanging their cloaks of green for ones of yellow, brown, red or gold, I surveyed the plunder I had accumulated during the long summer's virtually non-stop marauding. It was considerable. Like most Indians the Apache judged his wealth mainly in terms of horses. I had a herd of thirty. This made me very rich. I also possessed two excellent rifles, a shotgun, a revolver, several brightly woven Navajo blankets and a large quantity of jewelry and ornaments fashioned by skilled Mexican silversmiths.

As I stood beside the corral of branches and brushwood which contained the pony herd, my thoughts of Sagozhuni were shattered by a woman's scream. I turned and saw a beautiful Mexican girl dodging among the wickiups of the village. She was pursued by the ugly, bow-legged Zopilote. He had taken her during a recent attack on a large hacienda and had not yet succeeded in taming her.

Her running brought her closer to me. She was obviously trying to get among the horses and find a mount before Zopilote could catch her. She had much spirit but I had no desire to let anyone stampede the herd I had so carefully gathered during many months. So I stepped in front of her, not liking what I was doing, for I could now see many bruises upon her shapely, lithe body. She was clad only in the tattered remnants of an old American army shirt.

The other Apaches had collected in a bunch and were laughing at both the girl's discomfort and Zopilote's frustration. The inherent cruelty of these people — who were now as my own — had not reached me completely as yet, but there seemed to be little, if anything, I could do to prevent this girl taking another beating from her captor.

She stopped, wild-eyed with fear, as I stepped between her and her goal. She turned desperately and Zopilote slowed down to a shuffling walk as he saw that it was now impossible for her to reach the ponies. His misshapen mouth was distorted into what must have been intended as a look of triumph. He was gobbling excitedly. I felt sick.

She darted away again. But Cabeza had been standing quietly beside his lodge. Now he strode into the open and grabbed her arm. She fought like a cornered puma, all teeth and nails. But it was useless against Cabeza's magnificent strength. There was no warrior in the band his equal in hand-to-hand fighting. She quickly realized that there was no escape from this blue-eyed, bronze-skinned giant and immediately ceased to resist. Cabeza dragged her over to where I was standing and waited for Zopilote. The girl was trying to conceal her terror; but fear was written clearly upon her features.

Zopilote waddled over and eagerly thrust a hand towards the girl. She cowered back. Cabeza chopped his fist down hard on Zopilote's outstretched forearm. The ugly one, surprised, withdrew it and rubbed at it with his other hand to ease the pain.

Cabeza spoke in a low voice, heard only by the three of us. But the girl, now trembling visibly, did not understand the Apache tongue. "Cuchillo, hold her while I speak with my friend Zopilote." He pushed the girl into my arms but there was no more struggling from her. Her face now held a look of depressed resignation.

The other Apaches stayed where they were. They sensed that this was a personal thing between Cabeza and Zopilote. Only one person detached himself from the now silent group and strode over to us. And that was Coletto Negro.

He reached us in time to hear Cabeza tell Zopilote quietly yet ominously: "I want this woman. I will buy her from you or fight you for her. But I want her. Which is it to be?"

Coletto Negro interrupted. "She belongs to Zopilote," he said simply.

Cabeza turned to face the chief. "Yes, she is his slave. He beats and tried to use her in a manner which she desires not. She would not be my slave. I want her for my woman. For my wife. And for this I am prepared to give him many horses or fight him. The choice is his."

"But she is only a Mexican," protested Coletto Negro firmly. "This is how things are. They have always been taken as slaves."

"So was your son a Mexican at one time," returned Cabeza fiercely but without raising his voice. "Yet now he is a true Apache. Why should it be different for this woman?"

My father was silent for some time while Zopilote continued

to gibber unintelligibly. Finally, Coletto Negro spoke. "There can only be one answer to this," he said. "We will ask the woman herself."

Despite her ugly captor's protests the chief turned to the girl and asked in flawless Spanish: "To which of these two men do you wish to belong?" He looked first at Zopilote and then at Cabeza.

The girl's face relaxed. She walked across to Cabeza. "To him," she replied quietly.

"So be it," said the chief. He turned to Zopilote. "Do you wish to fight or accept the horses offered to you?" he demanded.

The ugly one always sounded foolish, but he was never a fool. He knew that he could not overcome Cabeza in fair combat. "The horses," he gobbled. "How many?"

"She is a beautiful woman," mused Coletto Negro. "I think that if she is worth a fight which could end in death then she should fetch at least ten horses."

Zopilote nodded greedily. Cabeza looked down at the lovely Mexican girl standing beside him and also nodded.

Still not content, Zopilote demanded that he be allowed to select the ponies himself from Cabeza's herd. The chief looked at the young warrior who nodded again.

His squat, bow-legged rival appeared satisfied but Coletto Negro warned him: "This thing ends here. If you attempt any form of reprisal against this young man or his woman then you will be punished according to the laws of this band."

Zopilote ambled happily over to Cabeza's pony herd. He was more than satisfied. With ten choice mounts in exchange for a Mexican captive, he had not lost face before his fellow braves and he had added considerably to his personal wealth. My father was a wise man.

Cabeza, although a contented man also, looked at me apologetically. "I am very sorry but there will be little stock of any quality left to help you win Sagozhuni once he has taken his pick."

"Do not worry, good friend," I countered. "If what I already possess is insufficient, then she cannot love me. And if this is so, then I do not want her. For I will not have her any other way. You understand?"

Cabeza looked down at the small supple figure now pressed close to him, with her head tilted backwards so that they could read what was in each other's eyes. "I understand," he answered quietly. Gently, he took hold of the girl's arm and led her towards his wickiup. My father smiled.

That night Coletto Negro ordered a wedding feast in their

honour to let his people know that this marriage between Cabeza and the Mexican girl, Dorita, unusual though it was, had their chief's approval.

# CHAPTER EIGHTEEN

My courtship of Sagozhuni was far more formal, for she was an Apache and there were rules. However, when one sees the way it is today, it is difficult, almost impossible, to believe that not until after my proposal did any words pass between us. Only smiles. Yet these looks told each of us all we wished to know concerning the other. Perhaps the speed with which I courted her was due, in part, to Cabeza's words which constantly invaded my mind: "There are plenty of young braves as eager to possess her as you are."

Such was Apache family life that, wherever the daughter was, there too was the mother. Sagozhuni and her mother, a tall, slim, dark-skinned woman with grey-flecked black hair bordering a narrow yet pleasant face, were no different from anyone else. They followed the custom religiously. Whether gathering food or working in and around the wickiup, they were always together. Even so at the various dances and other similar functions, which were the only occasions when maidens were allowed to mix socially with young warriors.

It was at such a dance that I first sensed Sagozhuni felt about me as I did about her. For, unlike similar occasions organized among white people, it was the girl who selected her partner from among the men; and not the man from among the women. And at this dance, Sagozhuni chose me. She walked across to me, with that slow dignity which I so greatly admired, and placed her hand gently on my shoulder. My stomach turned upside down and my heart beat hard and fast. She danced with no one else all evening. Yet we spoke not. But I could feel this wonderful sensation which was unlike any other I had ever known. I was sure she experienced it also. It was there in her eyes, as we shuffled back and forth in line with the other dancers to the monotonous, yet stirring, rhythmic pounding of the drums.

Raiding and hunting parties were frequent that year and I was too often away from the village; but there were no other honourable means by which an Apache could become a man of wealth. Despite these forced absences, however, I was able to attend two other dances that summer. And, again, on each occasion, Sagozhuni selected me as her dancing partner. As before, there were no words. They were not necessary. We both knew that this thing was strong between us. That there could be no casting it aside, even if we so wanted.

Now that I was certain how things were, I approached my father for his consent. He turned to his new wife, Gooyan (Lady of

Wisdom) whom he had married only recently, having loved his first wife dearly and mourned her death many years. "What do you think?" he asked her in playful seriousness. "Do you consider this boy capable of bearing the responsibilities that weigh heavy upon the shoulders of a married man?"

A little more than half her husband's age, Gooyan had an oval face with laughing eyes. "Not really," she giggled. "But it would mean that we would have the wickiup to ourselves should his proposal be accepted."

"What if the maiden he wishes to become his bride is choosy and rejects him?" countered my father. I felt acutely embarrassed by their banter but would have had it no other way as it indicated their fondness for me.

"Perhaps you are right," replied my stepmother. "But I think he should at least be permitted to ask her. She may be short-sighted and not see in him the defects which are so obvious to those with perfect vision."

"I see now how you earned your name," Coletto Negro told his wife. "These are indeed words of wisdom. My son, you have our consent." His voice became earnest in tone. "May Sagozhuni accept you and may you both know happy days and have many children."

I gasped. "You know the name of the one I wish to marry?"

There was a twinkle in my father's eyes. "Perhaps she is short-sighted my son but we are not."

My proposal to Sagozhuni was done in the manner of the Apache. Traditionally, a suitor would tie a number of horses, one, two, three or more, outside the wickiup of the maiden he desired to marry. The number of ponies he left there indicated two things. His degree of wealth and the measure of his love for the girl to whom he was offering marriage. The horses were left outside for a maximum of four days. If, during this time the maiden fed and watered them, it meant that his proposal had been accepted. If, however, she did not tend them at all throughout this period it meant that his suit had been unsuccessful. In which case he would untie his horses and take them back. A sad blow for the lover, but much worse for the horses which had been without food and water for four days.

Senor, you cannot imagine how hard my heart was pounding as I led and tethered eight of my best ponies outside Sagozhuni's lodge. Eight was a large number, but I loved her very much and wanted to impress her parents.

It was not considered correct for a girl to appear over-anxious to accept her suitor's proposal by caring for his animals on the first day. Neither was it thought right for her to allow them to remain unfed and unwatered for more than two days if she intended ultimate acceptance. Such behaviour was regarded as haughty and conceited.

Although I knew these things I was restless throughout the first day. I kept busy at various tasks in order to occupy my mind and prevent it from forcing my eyes to look towards the eight picketed and spirited mounts which were probably as uneasy as I was. They were not used to so confined an area of mobility. That night I slept not. As I lay fidgeting on my bed robes, every sound of the night became magnified many times over. The sweet song of a nocturnal bird became the screech of an angry eagle. The breeze that gently stirred the leaves of the trees became a hurricane threatening to uproot everything that stood in its path. I prayed fervently to Usen, the Creator of Life, that Sagozhuni would become my wife.

The morning's pale sunlight, slowly filtering its way through the interwoven brushwood of the wickiup roof, was a welcome sight. My taut body gradually relaxed. If I knew Sagozhuni as well as I thought I did, then today would bring me an answer. For I felt certain that she would not be so cruel as to leave the horses another full day without caring for them if she intended accepting my proposal. I arose and stepped outside to let the sun's warmth ease the stiffness from my body.

No one else was awake. The camp had the appearance of a present day ghost town. I felt like walking to help relax still further the tensions of mind and body which had built during the night. Not wishing to be seen anywhere near Sagozhuni's wickiup for fear of betraying my anxiety, I strolled leisurely in the opposite direction; towards the stream which rippled contentedly through the middle of the village.

My heart leaped. I was not alone with the dawn. Sagozhuni was leading two of my ponies to the water's edge.

The wedding feast lasted three days and nights. This was the custom among the Apaches. And one which was enjoyed by everyone; for they all liked to eat, drink and dance whenever an excuse arose. Throughout this time Sagozhuni and I were not permitted by tradition to speak with one another. I ate, drank and danced with the others but it was merely mechanical, for the strange stirring in the pit of my stomach was stronger than ever before. I looked across at Sagozhuni frequently. She was the most beautiful woman I had ever seen.

It was now the third night. From where I was seated I saw Sagozhuni looking steadily at me. I nodded. She stood up and slowly walked away from the circle of people still gorging themselves around a huge fire. The flames projected prancing shadows against the back of her white buckskin dress for a brief while. Then she was enveloped by the darkness behond the reach of firelight. This was the night when we were permitted to slip away from the others who would pretend not to see us leave.

In a concealed spot among the trees bordering the village was a temporary wickiup which I had erected. In this we would spend the first few days of our marriage.

Several minutes elapsed before I left to join Sagozhuni there. My heart was beating frantically against my ribs as if trying to break through them. Despite the food I had eaten, my stomach felt stretched and hollow. The palms of my hands were wet with perspiration. Is it not strange how a desirable woman can weaken a powerful man without touching him, whereas another man of strength might fight to his utmost limits and still not subdue him?

It was difficult to believe but there I was, about to join the woman I loved more than any other and who was now my wife, yet I felt an almost irrepressible urge to turn and run.

Sagozhuni must have heard me from within the wickiup for her voice came softly out to me. "Why do you not enter husband? Or have you had a change of heart?" she queried playfully. I smiled to myself, stopped and went inside.

Please excuse my tears, senor; but the good times, when they are no longer with us, become memories of sadness inextricably interwoven with happiness. Never did I know such times as those with Sagozhuni. And that first occasion was the happiest of them all. As I entered, I could smell the fragrance of the suds from the yucca plant's roots in which she had bathed her body. Then, in the glow cast by a small fire she had built, I saw her. A Navajo blanket of many beautiful colours was drawn up to her chin as she sat on the far side of the lodge. Her white buckskin dress lay on the ground beside her. The desire within my body was almost unbearable. I was wearing only a loin cloth and moccasins. The loin cloth was made of a flimsy material, as was the custom, for anything thicker would have been most uncomfortable in the heat of the desert. My physical urge must have been very obvious to her.

With one arm still holding the blanket across her body, she pointed with the other to a buffalo skin robe lying a few feet from her. I walked over and sat cross-legged upon it. There was an intense physical hunger for this woman clawing at my insides. I tried to conceal my eagerness.

After a few seconds, which became hours in my mind, she shrugged the blanket of many colours from her shoulders. It fell to the floor. Her body was exquisite. The skin was dark and smooth like rich brown silk. Her breasts were small with prominent nipples stiffened by the excitement which passed wordlessly between us. She came slowly over to me and I could smell the delicate perfume of the freshly crushed mint she had rubbed around them.

I took off my moccasins and fumbled with my loin cloth. She smiled, took hold of my wrists and shook her head. A feeling of astonishment swept through me. She had appeared so desirous, but now . . . then she gently began to remove the loin cloth herself.

It was a long, cold winter and, apart from occasional hunting parties, we seldom left the warmth of our lodges. By the time the spring sun was sufficiently strong to drive away the final traces of snow from our mountain camp, both Sagozhuni and Cabeza's wife, Dorita, were heavy with child. By the summer, Cabeza and I were fathers. We could not have been happier — for the children our wives had given us were sons. They would grow up together and become warriors together, we told each other proudly.

Cabeza had one advantage over me. He had no mother-in-law. It was not that an Apache mother-in-law caused any frictions between her daughter and the man she had married. In fact, many husbands in other societies would have welcomed, and still would welcome, the Apache system with great enthusiasm. For an Apache was never allowed to look upon or talk to his mother-in-law. This was extremely difficult, because once a man was married he left his own family for ever, and became a member of his wife's family group which, naturally, included his mother-in-law.

Domestic life for me consisted mainly of dodging and hiding. Even a man's wickiup and that of his wife's parents were built facing away from each other. I felt sorry for those men who chose to have more than one wife. Only when hunting or on the warpath was there any relief from this bizarre tradition — which I followed faithfully without ever knowing its origins.

The next six years were the happiest of my life. Cabeza and I spent much of our time teaching our sons to be strong in mind and body. It was a strict, even harsh, upbringing. But without it neither would have lived long into adulthood, for the Apache's existence was a continuous struggle between him and his environment. It gave him nothing. Whatever he wanted he had to fight for and if defeated he had to survive until the next encounter.

# CHAPTER NINETEEN

The winter of 1879 into 1880 was a bad one for us in the mountains. It lasted far longer than usual, and by the first signs of spring our supplies were virtually exhausted. The intense cold had made hunting forays practically impossible. And the few parties which had ventured out, found all game driven from the normal areas by the unusually low temperatures. Even the nearest Mexican settlement was too far away in such circumstances.

At the earliest indication of the improving weather conditions which announced the coming of spring, Coletto Negro sent out the largest hunting party I had seen during my many years with the band. Everyone was on the brink of starvation, and fresh meat was needed without delay if the weaker members, particularly the children and the elderly, were to survive. Even the horses were gaunt, with ribs showing clearly against their lean flanks, skins stretched across them like multi-coloured parchments. It had been a hard winter for them, also, and those which had fallen had immediately been butchered by the women and as quickly consumed by all. Nothing had been left. Not even the bones, hides and hooves. These had been boiled in melted snow to form a foul-smelling but nourishing soup.

The hunt was a success. The horses were laden with the carcasses of many deer; and one tough old mule found wandering among the foothills below our mountain camp. We had seen a family of bears but had left them undisturbed, for the Apache would not eat the meat of these animals. Neither would he eat the flesh of turkeys, pigs or fish. He had many superstitious beliefs concerning such creatures.

In fact the Apache had an unconquerable fear of anything he considered to be supernatural — and he believed that evil beings used certain animals, birds and natural forces as instruments for working spells. Thus he dreaded lightning flashes and unusual cloud formations, or encounters with bears, coyotes, snakes and above all, owls. To him the hooting of an owl was an omen of the very worst kind, for he was convinced that the spirits of dead people existed within these birds and that the hooting of one was a threat or warning from the spirit world.

Yet there was no owl's hoot to warn us of the tragedy that awaited us when we returned to the village. I have seen many terrible things in my life senor — but never have I seen such carnage. Women, children, old men, apprentice warriors and a handful of fighting men, more than a hundred in all, had been killed and

scalped. The bodies lay in grotesque positions; their raw skulls en-
crusted with patches of dried blood.

Terror clawed at my insides as I frantically searched among
the dead for Sagozhuni. I prayed to Usen that she had escaped the
slaughter. "Ai-yee!" I screamed. She had not. Neither had my son.
They lay sprawled side by side, her left hand still clutching his
clothing as if to prevent him being taken from her.

A few yards away Cabeza knelt beside the lifeless forms that
had once been his wife and son. He was sobbing quietly.

Coletto Negro had found the body of Gooyan. No tears ran
down his face but his eyes were filled with grief. And something
else. Something frightening to see in the eyes of any man. A look
that said everything. That said quite clearly that those responsible
for the slaughter would pay a terrible price.

When he spoke his voice was broken, yet still loud enough for
all to hear. "First we will bury our dead. Then we will search for
any who escaped the massacre, for all those we left behind are not
here now. If we find them alive they will tell us who did this
thing."

Please forgive me senor if I dwell but briefly upon what we saw
and felt, and the subsequent burial of the dead, but it was
something which still exists occasionally in my dreams at night
and causes me to awake sweating and trembling.

After the bodies were all buried, Coletto Negro ordered the
camp abandoned. "Burn everything." His voice was like the growl
of a wounded animal brought to bay by the hounds. But the
hunters of Apache scalps, for which the Mexican authorities paid
high bounties, would soon become the hunted. We all knew this.
We had lost everything other than the desire for revenge — and we
would follow our war leader no matter where the trail might take
us.

Many of us blamed ourselves for what had occurred. We knew
that the governing bodies of certain Mexican states offered bounties, in some cases as much as two hundred American dollars, for
each Apache scalp brought in. We raided their people frequently
and often killed many in the process, so the authorities wanted us
dead. And a scalp was proof enough that its previous owner had left
this earth. It was also far less weight to carry than the entire corpse.

But this legislation had been in operation many years and few
of our race had been scalped because of it. The simple reason being
that the average Mexican feared Apaches much more than he loved
money. He was philosophical. If a fellow Mexican was butchered
by Apaches, it was not his problem. And if he himself was killed,

then he no longer had any problems.

So we had grown complacent and careless, leaving but a few warriors to protect the camp while we were away hunting. Well, we would go hunting again. First to seek out any survivors of the massacre — and then to punish, according to Apache law, those responsible for it.

The tracks of those who had fled the slaughter were plain and easy to follow. They led southeast of the camp, along a thickly wooded cleft in the mountains towering around us.

After perhaps half a mile, we came across the bodies of three boys and two old men concealed behind boulders. They had obviously fought a rearguard action to cover the escape of the others. And they must have had some success for, although they were dead, they had not been scalped. Empty cartridge cases were scattered around them and, forty or fifty yards away, large dark stains upon the ground indicated clearly that many of the bullets from those cases had struck their targets. Scuff marks, in the earth and across the rocks, were evidence of dead or wounded men being dragged away.

These marks led to a clearing where a number of horses had been tethered to bushes. Leaves torn from these bushes, and the signs left by iron-shod hooves milling restlessly, told us this. Horse droppings, still faintly warm in the centre, said that the men we wanted were less than twelve hours distant. And they rode much slower than vengeful Apaches. A closer examination of the hoof prints signified twenty to twenty-five mounts. That meant, at the most, twenty-five riders, with some dead or dying.

Their trail would be easy to follow, and many of the warriors were eager to press on after the killers without any further delay. But others wanted to seek the survivors from among our own people before starting the pursuit. A heated argument erupted. Those who had found their entire families annihilated were for immediate action. Those who had not found all their loved ones among the dead, almost everyone had lost somebody, first wanted to learn the plight of those who still lived and to help them.

A slight rustling in the brush beyond the rocks behind which lay the five dead Indians, brought all words to an abrupt halt. Silently, Coletto Negro jabbed his right hand towards either side of the spot from whence came the sound. Silently the warriors encircled the area and slowly closed in.

A groan. Suddenly an Apache, of perhaps eighty summers, stumbled through the bushes and fell almost at our feet. The faded blue American army jacket which he wore, was stained a dark red across the chest. Coletto Negro knelt swiftly beside him. At first he appeared dead. Then he opened his eyes and there was recognition in them. He tried to sit up, but his chief placed a hand upon his shoulder to prevent this.

"Who did this?" asked Coletto Negro. "Mexicans?"

The old man shook his head. "Indah," he mumbled feebly. "Indah."

"White men!" Coletto Negro sounded surprised. "Americans?"

"Yes," replied the old man.

"Our people who still live. Where have they gone?"

But this time the chief's words were not heard by the old man. He was dead.

"You heard him," Coletto Negro told those gathered around him. "Americans!" He spat the word from between his lips like some distasteful object. "They will be in their own country before we can catch them."

"Perhaps not," said Lobo. "Maybe they will sell the scalps to the Mexican authorities before returning across the border." Several of the warriors nodded in agreement.

"Perhaps. But you can see which way their tracks lead. Directly northward. And there is no town between here and the border. I think they are afraid because they were unable to kill all in our village and think that some of the survivors rode out to meet us."

"But why should they think this?" interrupted a tall, lean brave standing behind Coletto Negro. "How do they even know of our existence?"

The chief turned impatiently to face this man. "Because, foolish one, their attack on our camp was planned so well. It was not a thing of chance. Twenty or so men would never dare to attack such a large village without first ensuring that the fighting men were not there in any force. No, they watched us go, waited a while, perhaps one or two of them even followed us for a short distance, and then they struck. But some of our people escaped. The Americans, fearing our return, fled with what scalps they had. Later, some of them will return to Mexico to claim the bounties for which they killed those whom we loved."

There was great logic in what he had said and for a brief time no one spoke. Then Cabeza asked: "What would you have us do then? For it is now obvious to us all, I think, that we shall never catch these men. How can we allow such a terrible crime to remain unpunished?"

86

"It will not go unpunished," returned the chief, his voice a low growl from between clenched teeth. For several minutes he said nothing further, his eyes expressionless, staring into the distance as if looking for the answer in some place inaccessible to the rest of us. We waited silently for him to return from this place.

His eyes suddenly became alive again, and those of us closest to him knew that he had found the answer. "They cared not whom they slew," he said. "Women, children, old men. It mattered not to them. Neither will it concern us whom we kill as long as they are Americans. We will find those of our people who are still alive. We will leave them food and also warriors to protect and provide for them.

"Then the rest of us will cross the border to the land that was once our own. There we will kill as many white-eyes as we can before the soldiers force us back here into Mexico. It will be a raid that will forever live in the minds of the Americans who afterwards see the bodies of all who come into our hands. For their dying will not be easy."

I looked quickly around at my fellow warriors. There was excitement on their faces and in their voices.

"What about plunder?" demanded the greedy Zopilote who had lost no one during the massacre of our people, having no one to lose.

"Horses. Only horses," was Coletto Negro's immediate reply, "For we must travel swiftly and, therefore, lightly. We will carry little food or water, but will live off the land as we did in the old days. The water holes in the desert will not have moved and the Americans, although unwillingly, will supply us with food and whatever else we may require. Now, let us look for those who fled the camp and are still living so that we can fill their empty stomachs."

Their tracks were easy to follow. For these were not battle-hardened warriors carefully erasing their back trail as they moved, but panic-stricken women, children and old men fleeing from a pack of merciless white butchers.

When we found them they were huddled together in a small arroyo about five miles from the village. There were no more than forty left alive. The women had cut their hair short as a sign of mourning for loved ones now dead. Old men and young boys, ancient firearms, bows and arrows clasped tightly in their hands, stood ready to make one last desperate stand.

All were pitiful to see. Already reduced to near starvation by the terrible winter, the flight on foot had also left its marks upon them. Their clothes hung in shreds, ripped by the thorny brush through which they had fled. The sharp rocks had cut deeply into their moccasins. and some were without footwear at all, their feet covered only by layers of congealed blood.

# CHAPTER TWENTY

The preparations for the raid north into the United States were thorough. Coletto Negro decided to take only fifty men with him. The remainder were to stay in Mexico to protect and feed what was left of the band. The last I ever saw of these people was when they set out to find a new camp deeper in the mountains. They looked completely dejected as they trudged away with what few possessions remained to them. Warriors flanked them on either side. Those too injured, crippled or sick to walk were placed upon travois dragged by a motley handful of scrawny ponies. All other mounts were rquired by those fighting men who would soon ride northward. Babies were strapped to their mothers' backs in a type of cradle which the Apaches call a tsach. Theirs were the last faces I saw as the band moved into the distance.

Coletto Negro immediately held a brief war council. There would be no set plan other than to strike isolated ranches and homesteads, parties of travellers and small settlements in a series of hit and run attacks. All large towns and military outposts were to be avoided. Encounters with mobile army units, particularly cavalry, were also to be avoided wherever possible. The chief wanted to keep his elite fighting force as intact as possible.

With this desire foremost in his mind, he summoned the shaman, Aguila, now also turned warrior to avenge his wife and three children killed during the massacre, to perform the medicine rituals which preceded all forays made by war paries. The brief rites ended with Aguila throwing a small amount of hoddentin towards the sun.

Hoddentin was the sacred pollen of the tule, cattail, and was a powerful medicine among the Apache people. It was used in most religious ceremonies. We all carried some in small bags of buckskin — much like superstitious soldiers who will not go into battle without their good luck charms or amulets. Apart from its magical properties, however, hoddentin was also credited with other qualities. It was used in cases of sickness, when it would be eaten, and in times of exhaustion, when a warrior would place a pinch of it upon his tongue to replenish lost energy.

Many of us also wore brightly decorated medicine shirts which, it was believed, provided protection for their wearers against enemy bullets and arrows.

Unlike Juan Caballo, the medicine man he had succeeded, Aguila was far more realistic. Magic alone was not enough, he told us. There would be certain dangerous situations which he could not foresee and could not, therefore, counteract in advance. This raid should not be one of heated impetuosity but of cold reasoning. "In this way alone can we find the revenge we seek."

We were all mounted on wiry Indian ponies, small yet renowned for their endurance. Unencumbered by the amount of equipment that an American cavalry unit was forced to bring into the field, we could cover daily more than twice the distance of which the soldiers were capable. Twenty-five miles a day was supposed to be their limit. Some days they managed as many as forty. Yet we could travel more than eighty miles with comparative ease in the same time. The army's main advantages lay in its great numerical superiority, the pincer-like tactical movements which became possible with such huge forces and the tremendous firepower of its large field guns.

Against such awesome odds we had only speed, endurance, the skills of a people that had survived for centuries by war alone, individual fitness and, most important, a far stronger mental attitude coupled with an insatiable desire to kill. These things appear very small in cold conversation but, in the heat of action, they assume far greater size. We knew they were more than enough.

Each one of us carried a quantity of mescal, made from the maguey plant, and dried meat. These were a good diet for warriors. All were armed with guns. Not one lance or bow was in evidence. We had only a small remuda of spare horses — but this increased steadily as we moved towards the border. The Mexicans from whom we took these additional mounts never once complained. This was because we were in a hurry and always killed them before plundering their ranches and homes. They were fortunate. At another time many would have been tortured slowly to death. It was their government which had offered the scalp bounties.

In less than a day we were back in our former homeland. For me it was the first time in fifteen years. We crossed the border near the source of the Rio San Pedro and moved cautiously eastwards, camping the night in the eastern foothills of the Dragoon Mountains. Although darkness provides excellent cover for attacks by small bands of marauders such as we were, the Apache would never fight at night unless faced with no alternative. He believed that should he be killed at such a time, his spirit would walk in darkness for eternity. So we waited impatiently for the dawn.

The vast American Southwest, particularly Arizona and New Mexico, was, and still is, an area of wild, unparalleled magnificence. But when the heart is filled with hatred, the eye sees no beauty. And so it was with us the following morning, as the climbing sun cast its weird, slowly changing patterns and colours across the country spread before us. There was no nostalgia in returning. This was no longer our home. It was home of the pinda lick-o-yi, the white eyes, the people we had come to kill.

That part of the Southwest through which Coletto Negro made his historic raid, I speak of eastern Arizona and western New Mexico, was friendly to the Apaches but unfriendly to the white-eyes. It is a region of nothing and, yet, everything. A desolate land of infrequent rains, sparse vegetation and seldom-seen wildlife. But with an unmatched grandeur in its natural structures and an unbelievable variety of colours, shapes and patterns in the plants and wildlife which are peculiarly its own.

We knew this country like a farmer knows the land on which he works and lives. We knew every waterhole, spring, stream, canyon, arroyo, mountain and valley. Once the food we carried was no more, we would be able to survive in this arid wilderness as did its animals, birds and reptiles. The Apache could subsist on a diet of berries, edible plants and even pack rats dug from their desert burrows.

White people, however, with few exceptions, were happiest where there were roads between neighbours, frequent places in which to eat and drink along such highways, and large settlements where they could sell their produce, buy their requirements and enjoy life a little before returning home.

But that summer of 1880 the region was still young to the white-eyes; and such comforts were very few and widely separated. Yet many Americans chose to live there in virtual isolation. Sometimes it was for the gold, silver and other minerals to be found in many parts, in other cases it was to establish lonely trading posts along the few routes which traversed that great land, and, in some instances even, to carve out small ranches or homesteads.

The miners, traders, ranchers, farmers and travellers. Wherever the situation was to our advantage, these would be the people among whom we would find vengeance for our dead. It would not be difficult, for the country was far too large to be adequately patrolled by the pony soldiers. And even if they saw us, they would never catch us.

After a cold breakfast we rode steadily northwards. Scouts, with Lobo as their leader, were sent ahead to seek out any small pockets of settlers or bands of travellers. Also to keep us informed of any army movements, as we were well aware that our presence in the area could not remain unnnoticed indefinitely. To do this they would either leave rows of stones, indicating the military's strength and situation, or flash pieces of mirror or shiny metal in the sun. This last method, similar to the army's heliograph system, was the most commonly employed. I never once saw an Apache war party make use of smoke signals.

Smoke was too slow. And the rows of stones were only employed when there was no immediate danger and we were concealed from the scouts. It was merely a means of conveying general information concerning any signs left by army patrols no longer in the vicinty. In times of urgency it was always the glass or metal mirror reflecting the light of the ever-present sun.

Coletto Negro had devised an elementary, but effective, code for use by his advance scouts. Two flashes, repeated at intervals, indicated the military. Four flashes, civilian quarry. If the final reflection in any sequence came from a mirror being slowly lowered, then the soldiers or civilians were heading towards us. A gradually rising last flash meant they were moving away from us. And people to our right or left were indicated by the final flash in any set crossing in the appropriate direction.

But on that first day there were no flashes. No enemy. Only us and the land. The land. Before nightfall we had covered more than fifty miles of rocky desert plateau, cut by sudden gorges and clad briefly by the towering saguaro cactus and the occasional stunted mesquite tree. The distant Chiricahua Mountains, many miles to our right, showed grey on the lower levels and green higher up. The sun was merciless — but to warriors with even less pity in their hearts, the terrible heat went practically unnoticed. Nevertheless, the coolness of the night was refreshing and, therefore, welcome.

Even for Apaches we were travelling at a very fast pace. By noon of the following day we had covered perhaps forty miles. The weaker horses were showing a great deal of stress. But they would be ridden until they fell. Then they would be killed and most of the flesh eaten uncooked by the hungry warriors. The entrails of the dead animals would then be wrapped around the fresh mounts from the remuda, and used as water carriers immediately the opportunity came to fill them.

By mid afternoon the first pony had succumbed and was dispatched immediately. But it was only a brief respite and we were soon moving again, chewing on pieces of raw, still warm, horseflesh and offal.

The heat was oppressive and a variety of winged insects were always ready to alight in swarms upon us, and on our mounts, whenever we slowed down sufficiently or stopped. No amount of brushing or slapping prevented them from inflicting their vicious little bites. They were a source of constant irritation.

We were now passing through areas of cholla, prickly pear, ironwood, barrel cactus, creosote bush, yucca, ocotillo, agave, cottonwood, sagebrush, chapparal, mesquite and the sentinel-like saguaro which continued to maintain its lofty vigil on all horizons. Through country hardened and cracked by the heat and other natural processes of God knows how many years. Occasionally, the countless wrinkles which creased the scarred and pitted face of this ancient land would reveal small animals like the bobcat and peccary; and even smaller species such as the rats and mice of the desert. Sometimes vividly coloured, uniquely patterned snakes and lizards and, less frequently, scorpions and tarantulas. But no white-eyes. The search continued.

The sun was more than half-way along its daily downhill run when the flashes were first seen. They were coming in groups of four. Civilians. Then the small patch of dazzling brightness moved slowly upwards. A party of Americans heading north, away from us. There was little chance of us catching up with them before nightfall, but our tired mounts now moved faster as we viciously jabbed our heels into their flanks.

Although the flashes had appeared close, more than an hour passed before we were up with our scouts. One of them, A stocky young man called Garanon, the stallion, by the Mexicans because of his ways with captive women, spoke to Coletto Negro. "White-eyes. Four men with a wagon. Travelling slowly. Perhaps four or five miles ahead by now."

His words were greeted with an eager excitement. The fighting men at once commenced chattering like over-enthusiastic schoolboys who had just discovered an entirely new toy or pastime. Only the chief and those closest to him remained silent for perhaps two or three minutes.

"Well, my chief, do we strike them now?" asked an impatient young brave of eighteen or nineteen summers.

"I think not," replied Coletto Negro. "Darkness will be with us in a short time."

Howls of protest came from several warriors.

Ignoring them the chief turned to the scout, Garanon. "These men. How do they look?" he asked. "How are they armed?"

"They look like men who know well how to fight," replied the scout. "Each carries a revolver in his belt and a repeating rifle in his hands. They are alert for trouble and the wagon would give them excellent cover. If we attack them openly without any preconceived strategy, then many of us will be killed before we kill them."

Anxious to keep his band as intact as possible for the long series of hit and run raids ahead of them, Coletto Negro taunted: "Well, my eager warriors, how do you feel now that you have heard the words of Garanon? How many of you are ready for the world of darkness beyond death which awaits all who die at night?"

The braves were quickly silent. The chief had made his point. Now, he spoke again: "Garanon will lead us to these men. We will plan our ambush well and at the first light of dawn they will all die. This I promise."

Garanon was sent ahead to scout the Americans' night camp. After some time he reappeared as suddenly and silently as he had departed. Without a word he wheeled his mount around and moved once more into the darkness. This time we followed.

Although the Apaches were great horsemen, they preferred to fight on foot. So, when we were still a mile or so away from the Americans' camp the young scout reined his pony to a halt, turned and spoke briefly to Coletto Negro. The chief signalled for us to dismount. Our horses were herded together by the five braves who would guard them until we returned. A cold meal of dried meat was followed by an even colder night, for the chief allowed no fires to betray our presence.

With still two or three hours until daybreak, Coletto Negro made his move. Each man was awakened and immediately checked his weapons. Then, like so many phantoms, we drifted noiselessly into the night. As with all other people the Apache could not see where there was total darkness. But, unlike most people, wherever there was the faintest trace of light he had the eyes of a cat. Very few nights in the desert, where the skies are normally cloudless, are without some light from the moon and stars; so it was a simple task for us to surround the white-eyes' camp. There to wait for the dawn and our chief's signal to attack.

The small fire burned steadily a short distance from the wagon. Three figures lay sprawled asleep around it. The fourth man sat with his back against a wagon wheel. He was in the shadows but he was not asleep for, occasionally, his head would move slightly to the right or left as if he was peering into the darkness beyond the reach of the firelight. The almost imperceptible tilt of his head at any unusual sound, no matter how faint, showed that keen sense of hearing which comes only to those who have travelled the wilderness for many years. A repeating rifle rested across his outstretched legs. His hands held the gun in such a manner that it could be brought into a firing position very quickly. His three companions had similar weapons alongside them.

As the time crawled slowly and painfully by, I wondered if any of my fellow warriors were experiencing thoughts similar to my own. Here were four seasoned men not only ready, but also obviously well able, to fight for their lives at a moment's notice. It would be a bad thing for any of our people to be killed, or even injured, during this first attack. We were a superstitious race and many would feel that any such happening would forebode ill for the rest of the raid. This was no time to attempt to take prisoners for torturing, I thought. This was a time for killing only. A time for creating confidence, not destroying it.

With this in mind, I moved stealthily among the rocks and brush ringing the camp until I found Coletto Negro. He was surprised to see me but said nothing. I told him quietly of my thoughts. Many seconds passed before he answered me. "You are right my son," he whispered. "Select eight good marksmen. I want two rifles aimed at each white-eye. When I give the signal they must shoot to kill. Tell them I want it so because I do not desire to lose good fighting men. Go."

I moved swiftly and without sound, picked my eight men and awaited Coletto Negro's signal. It came with the very first glow of dawn. The Americans never knew what happened. They were all dead within seconds. The expected protests never came from those warriors who had been unaware of the altered plan, for someone quickly discovered that the wagon was loaded with repeating rifles and ammunition.

Coletto Negro smiled as he patted one of the new rifles, cradled lovingly in his arms like a newly born son. "This is good," he told himself softly. "Very good." Suddenly aware that I was beside him he turned to me. "You think well," he said. "Although they would obviously disagree with me, were they in a position to do so." He indicated the four dead men. "They will sell no more guns to the Apache or any other tribe."

"You know them?"

"No. But I have seen them before, trading their firearms for many horses and furs with the Apache, the Comanche, the Navajo and other Indian peoples. That is why they were so vigilant. They were not afraid of us; only of the pony soldiers who could have punished them terribly if they had caught them selling guns to the Indians." He laughed cynically. "That is funny."

"What is?"

"Killing these men. By doing so we help the soldiers. There would have been many more wagon loads of guns for our people if we had allowed the white-eye renegades to live. But now they are dead and will bring no more guns."

For some time he stood in thoughtful silence. "Perhaps it is a good thing for the Apache and all other Indians that we did what we did," he said quietly after a while.

"I do not understand," I told him.

"My son, these men gave us weapons in exchange for horses which they then sold to the pony soldiers. We used the white-eye guns to shoot at the soldiers while they chased us on Indian ponies. It was madness. Now it is ended."

"Why is such a thing good for all Indians, as you say it is?" I asked him. I was very puzzled. "We can always get ponies to replace the ones we trade. But guns are much more difficult to obtain."

For the first time ever I saw a look of weary acceptance in Coletto Negro's eyes. Suddenly he looked older. I noticed the wrinkles lining his face and the many silver hairs intermingled with the black on his head. "I have fought the white-eyes for many years now," he replied. "Too many I think. Every time you kill one of them, ten more spring up to take his place. Yet each time they kill one of our warriors, there is no one to replace him. It can end in one way only; defeat for all Indian peoples everywhere. Already most tribes are living on reservations allotted to them by the white-eye chiefs. There is no alternative path for the Indian other than death."

"Then, tell me. Why do we go on this raid? Why do we continue to fight if only to lose in the end?"

The chief straightened to his full height. "Because we are Apaches," he answered proudly. "We will lose as a people. But this raid will be successful. We will honour our dead as we promised. That is our way. It has always been so. Afterwards, who can say? Perhaps peace in Mexico. Perhaps not. Each one must make his own choice. But, for me, to die as a warrior is much better than to live like a caged animals. I will never live on a reservation. Never! Come! We must return to our ponies and search for more white-eyes."

# CHAPTER TWENTY-ONE

It was well into the afternoon before we again saw any flashes. As we approached the spot from which they came, Lobo, in charge of the scouts, pointed to a small valley perhaps a half-mile distant. It was dotted with sheep and their bleating came to us clearly through the dry, still air.

"How many men?" Coletto Negro asked him tersely.

"Three," replied Lobo. "Mexicans," he added contemptuously.

"We will take them alive," said Coletto Negro. He pointed to eight battle-hardened warriors. "You will signal once you have them." The men dismounted and moved swiftly and silently in the direction of the sheepherders' camp. Not even the dogs guarding the sheep heard their coming.

The chief looked down at the three cringing Mexicans now on their knees before him begging for their lives. But there was no mercy in his eyes and, even as they pleaded, they knew that it was useless. There was a fearful resignation written clearly on their faces.

"Tie them while we eat," ordered Coletto Negro. "There is no hurry." He looked across the valley. It was green and looked a place of peace, not violence. The sheep, two or three hundred of them, continued grazing. A narrow, shallow stream, bordered by clumps of aspen, juniper, pinon and willow trees, lazily snaked its way through the meadowland surrounding it.

"Kill the sheep!" commanded the chief. "But do not waste bullets. Save them for the white-eyes."

Sheep are stupid creatures. They simply milled around helplessly while the warriors clubbed and knifed them to death. Some fell, bleeding, into the stream in their frantic efforts to escape the slaughter. The water became streaked with crimson. The Apaches revelled in the killing, laughing as they did it. To me it was a senseless thing. I had come to kill men, not sheep. So I did not join in. Neither did Cabeza. He came over to me.

"Well, Cuchillo my friend, why are you not enjoying yourself together with our brothers?" he asked.

"Because I find no joy in such killing," I answered. "And you? What is your reason?"

"The same. What they are doing makes no sense to me. It is a waste." He grinned wryly. "Perhaps there still remains something of the farmer inside me which I cannot be rid of. Who knows?"

I was somewhat startled by his words. This was the first time since we were boys together that he had referred to his background.

It made me thoughtful and I asked myself: Is it the same with me?

Any further conjecture was interrupted by Coletto Negro, now standing silently a few paces behind us. "These men will be hungry when they are finished," he said, indicating the warriors who were still striking in all directions as they strode among their woolly victims. He pointed to a group of five tethered mules, obviously used by the sheepherders as mounts and pack-animals. "Butcher them," he ordered. "I will make their owners light fires and cook the meat for us." There was a cruel smile on his face.

He walked over to the three captives, cut them loose and spoke to them in Spanish. They were too far away for me to hear what he said, but the Mexicans hurriedly commenced gathering wood, frequently glancing backwards as they collected the fuel for the cooking fires. If they were worried about being shot down from behind I could have allayed such fears, substituting worse ones. Their dying would not be easy. For some reason this disturbed me.

Cabeza's hand touched my shoulder. "Come," he said. "At least there is sense and no waste in killing for food."

A delicacy among Apaches at any time, mule meat was even more delicious when it was the first cooked food eaten in four days. The sheepherders, once again tied together, sat silent and afraid. One was quietly mouthing a prayer to his God. Sweat glistened on their foreheads. It was not the perspiration brought on by the heat of the fire or the exertion of woodgathering. But by absolute terror.

Suddenly I felt a great sympathy for them. Why? Their people had offered rewards for the scalps of my people so why feel sorry for them. No, not their people, but the government of a country they had left. A government which abused its own peons as much as it did any Apache. That was why I felt sympathy for them. You cannot blame the people of any one race for the bad things committed by others of the same race. This was wrong.

This was why my own wife and son had been murdered. They had been killed for things which occurred long before they were born. A chain of events which reached back hundreds of years into the past when the Apaches killed their first Spaniard or the Spaniards killed their first Apache. Who knows which way it happened? These depressing thoughts would not leave my mind and the meat became tasteless. I ate only to restore my energy for the arduous miles ahead.

"Let us finish this mule meat quickly. There is other flesh for us to cut." The voice was that of Sagozhuni's father, Jayan, who had lost not only his daughter to the scalphunters but also his wife.

It was the first time I had heard him speak since we had discovered the bodies. I looked at him. The dignity had gone from his face. In its place was the look of a wild animal. His arms were covered in dried blood. He had liked killing the sheep but he would enjoy even more the torturing of the herders.

Coletto Negro nodded. Like a pack of hounds suddenly let loose, the warriors grabbed the three Mexicans, stripped them naked and tied them by their wrists and ankles to stakes driven into the ground. They lay there screaming for mercy, arms and legs so stretched that each man resembled a grotesque four-pointed star. Tears channelled their way through the grime of their faces.

Jayan took out his skinning knife and squatted on his haunches beside one of the terrified Mexicans. With a single slash he cut off that part of a man which makes him a man. The sheepherder shrieked in agony like a wounded mountain lion. Jayan laughed and dangled the peon's amputated manhood above his face. The screams from all three captives grew louder and tore at my ears and my soul.

In that short time I knew I could never be truly an Apache. Looking across at Cabeza, I could see no pleasure in his eyes either. His teeth bit deeply into his lower lip. He saw the expression on my face and we both knew how it was. Killing was a necessary part of the Apache's fight for survival and we accepted it. Just as I accepted the desire, still strong within me, to avenge the deaths of my wife and son. And I would kill. But not in this manner. For what our brother warriors were doing was wrong.

The unfortunate wretches staked out before us writhed in pain as the knives sliced little pieces from their naked bodies. Their shrill cries tore apart the tranquility of the valley. "For the love of God!" screamed one. "For the love of God make it quick!" But the Apaches laughed and continued their savage butchery; for the death of the cuts was never quick.

The raid continued. A long succession of terrified screams, contorted faces and mutilated bodies. Sounds and sights that would not leave my mind. Not even at night when I slept. This was not the way I had thought it would be when we had first set out. That there would be torture I had known. But not like this. I was sickened by it all. Even the desire to kill had left me. I was like a man trapped in the rapids of a swift-flowing river; wanting to get out but not knowing how.

Within a period of nine days we had travelled nearly five hundred miles, killed more than forty people and captured perhaps three or four hundred horses. They were slowing us down, but horses represented great wealth to the Apache. To him they were as gold to the white-eyes.

On the morning of the tenth day signals came yet again from the scouts ahead. But, for the first time since we commenced the raid, the flashes came in pairs. The military! The final flash moved away to our left. We looked in that direction and saw a small dust cloud. It was moving towards us.

The chief ordered a halt and waited for the scouts to rejoin us.

Lobo was the first to do so. His mount was breathing heavily. "Pony soldiers," he told Coletto Negro. "Perhaps a hundred. At least double our number. They have Indian scouts with them. These scouts are following our trail. But the soldiers are moving slowly so they cannot have seen us yet."

The chief looked towards the dust cloud. It was perhaps four or five miles distant and, as Lobo had stated, moving slowly. We were in the high plateau region of northeast Arizona. The soldiers were well below us. Our trail up to the plateau was across rocky terrain and would be difficult to follow. And the climbing would slow down the heavily equipped cavalry.

Coletto Negro made his decision quickly. We would cross into New Mexico through the Canyon de Chelly. Although not a difficult path it would slow the soldiers nevertheless for they would fear a possible ambush. As we drove the stolen horses through the canyon, scouts were sent to the rear as well as to the front. After a day's hard drive the rearguard reported that we had shaken off our pursuers. That night was spent in a small arroyo a short distance from Chaco Canyon.

We were awake early the following morning and, after a cold breakfast, were quickly in the saddle. Once again scouts were sent to the front and rear. And also on both flanks. We were now moving south again. To Mexico, I hoped.

But, gradually, we veered to the southeast, and I knew then that the raid was not over and that the chief would kill many more white-eyes before we returned home. With this knowledge came a feeling of unease. For now that the military authorities obviously were aware of our presence in their country, I felt strongly that some of us would die also. To date we had suffered no casualties. From here in, however, the time that we remained north of the border was not our own. It was borrowed. The American soldiers were slow but their chiefs were not stupid. Even now, without a doubt, they were trying to trap us. More than ever before there was a need for constant vigilance.

Another hard day's drive but without incident of any kind.

That night we camped near the source of the San Jose River.

The next day was the hottest of the entire raid. The sun was a circular opening, showing white hot, in a bright blue furnace. Dust from the horses' hooves hung in a dense grey cloud in the windless air. A cloud which stung the eyes and made breathing difficult. Only those riding in front were free of the choking, blinding dust. Only they saw the signals on our left flank. Flashes which told of civilians travelling northeast towards Santa Fe.

To intercept them we had to change direction again. This time we rode due east. The scouts who had signalled us, Garanon and his younger brother, Espejo, looking glass, so called because of his expertise in the use of the mirror for signalling, pointed along the deep-rutted tracks that were the road to Santa Fe. "A coach," said Garanon. "Five white-eyes. Two men on top. Two women and a pony soldier chief inside."

"Enju — it is well!" grunted Coletto Negro and urged his pony at a gallop along the route taken by the stagecoach. The rest of us followed close on his heels. It was a fast yet brief pursuit. The wildly rocking vehicle was quickly overtaken.

Then the chief made his first mistake of the raid and we suffered our first casualties. The man seated beside the driver on top of the swaying coach had a twin-bore shotgun grasped firmly in his hands. In his desire to take all five people alive Coletto Negro chose to ignore the man and his gun. It was a fatal error. Immediately we were alongside the coach the guard swung the shotgun towards us and fired both barrels into our midst. Three braves tumbled from their mounts.

There was an immediate return of fire from the fallen warriors' comrades. The guard and driver were dead before they struck the ground.

A small group of us cut in front of the runaway team of horses and brought the vehicle to a halt. The doors were wrenched open and the occupants pulled roughly from inside. Garanon had been right. Two women and a pony soldier chief. The cavalry officer looked familiar to me.

"Glencoe," said Lobo in quiet satisfaction. Of course. Now I knew. This was the officer who had ordered his men to fire upon our people and had driven us into Mexico many years before. His paunch was even bigger and his black beard was streaked with grey. But this was the man.

Lobo addressed him in the white man's tongue. "I told you one day I kill you Glencoe. This is that day." He turned to two men. This time he spoke in Apache. "Tie him to a wheel of the coach. But do not hurt him. He is mine. Anyone who harms him will have to fight me — to the death." No one was eager to take up the challenge as Lobo was still a renowned fighter. Glencoe was dragged, protesting, to the coach and tied to one of its wheels by the wrists.

All this time the two women were struggling and screaming as they were passed from warrior to warrior. Each man in turn ripped a piece of clothing from the hysterical captives until they were completely naked. It was the custom to rape women prisoners. Most of the men were eagerly taking off their breech clouts.

"Not yet!" barked Coletto Negro. "Have you forgotten those who were shot from their horses?"

Shamefaced, several of the men replaced their breech clouts and rode back to where the men had fallen. The rest waited. The women must have known it was only a temporary reprieve but they were strangely silent. I looked at their faces. There was still fear written there; yet even clearer was the look of resignation in their eyes.

Those who had ridden off to bring back the three braves blasted by the guard's shotgun now returned grim-faced. Two of the men were dead and the third was wounded in the right side. It was bleeding freely.

"Bury them," said Coletto Negro quietly, pointing to the two dead warriors slung across their ponies.

While this was being done the medicine man, Aguila, bound the fleshy parts of leaves from the thorny nopal plant to the side of the injured brave. These would aid the healing of the wound, The man, I cannot recall his name, was obviously in pain but he kept it within him.

The warriors once again turned their attention to the two women. But this time neither of them fought, or even cried out, as they were thrown to the ground. One of them, tall with hair the colour of dried grass, turned to her companion lying on the hot earth beside her. "Hell, they're only men honey. Just open your legs and try to smile. The only difference is that this time we ain't gettin' paid."

Cabeza translated her words for me and we both knew that neither of them was a woman of breeding.

The other, shorter, somewhat plump and with brown hair, forced a grin. But behind it I could see a terrible fear building up inside her. I did not take part in what followed. Neither did Cabeza and a few others. I did not desire even to watch. Yet a horrible fascination would not allow me look away.

One after another, grunting like animals, the men who had been my companions for so long, thrust their foul-smelling, sweaty, grimy bodies upon the naked women beneath them. As each spent his passion he would roll off to enable another to take his place.

The short woman with brown hair suddenly screamed. The ugly, pock-marked Zopilote was about to take his turn with her. But it was too much for her. He was probably the ugliest man she had ever seen. She continued to scream.

The other warriors began to laugh at Zopilote's obvious embarrassment as the woman struggled beneath him. Without warning he reached for his knife on the ground beside him, stuck it between her legs and slit her open to the waist. She died, bleeding profusely and shrieking in agony.

The tall one beside her fainted. Yet the men continued to take her as if nothing had occurred. Even Zopilote. After a while her eyes opened again. But they were completely vacant. Still the braves kept taking her, until her eyes closed again. This time they would not re-open. She was dead. Inside, I felt sick, like a man who had eaten bad food.

Ignoring the two bodies on the ground, the warriors now turned towards Glencoe. He was wrestling furiously with the rawhide thongs which bound him to the wheel. But it was futile. Lobo smiled at him. A smile as evil as a rattlesnake and as cold as winter.

"You cannot do this to me!" blustered Glencoe. "Every soldier in the army will be looking for you if you kill me. I am not just any soldier. I am no longer a major but a general."

"You get promoted?" grinned Lobo. "Good for you. But even if I no kill you, soldiers still come. So I kill. I do not like break promise to friend."

Tears rolled down Glencoe's cheeks as Lobo held the officer's hair firmly in one hand and poured gunpowder into his mouth with the other.

Lobo saw the tears and spat in Glencoe's face in disgust. "You not general. You not even soldier. Cry like baby. Not die like man."

His next words were in Apache. "Set fire to the coach!" he commanded. Three or four warriors hastened to the task. The wooden body of the vehicle was soon blazing. Glencoe's eyes rolled wildly; but the powder cramming his mouth prevented sounds other than grunts. The flames began to lick at his face. There was an explosion. When the smoke cleared his body still sagged against the burning coach. But his head had gone.

Somewhere among the warriors a fight suddenly started. The chief shouldered his way through the jostling braves until he came to the two combatants. I followed him. Jayan was struggling furiously with Espejo for possession of the shotgun dropped by the guard when he was blasted from the top of the coach. It was a fine weapon. Both men were perspiring freely. There was a look of terrible madness in Jayan's eyes. Before any of us could move to stop him he snatched a knife from his belt and plunged it into Espejo's stomach.

The young warrior immediately dropped the shotgun. Clasping his hands across the jagged wound made by the blade, he slumped to the earth. His mouth opened as if to speak but was filled with bloody froth. A few seconds later he was dead.

Jayan had picked up the gun and was holding it tightly. "It is mine. It is mine," he kept saying.

Coletto Negro stared at him coldly. "There will be a trial," he said.

"What? Now?" asked a brave.

"Yes, now!" the chief replied curtly. "I want no bad blood among us when we ride. For this reason it will be settled here."

Apache justice was swift, yet fair. There were no long-winded speeches as in the white man's courts. No known liars were permitted to give evidence. Witnesses of any incident gave their evidence briefly; and those in judgment gave their verdict.

On this occasion there were many witnesses. All told the same story. Espejo had found the gun at the place where the guard had dropped it and had brought it with him. Seeing it, Jayan had first asked Espejo for it and then offered to trade. When the latter had refused, Jayan had taken it by force, killing Espejo in the process. Coletto Negro had no choice. The verdict was obvious. It was but a formality. The accused was guilty of murder. Among a people noted for its killing this was, as strange as it may appear, a terrible crime.

Then the chief passed sentence. He gave Jayan two alternatives. Banishment from the tribe; this was considered to be a punishment worse than death, for the banished man was not allowed to join any other tribe and could live only with those of his kind. Thus were renegade bands born. Geronimo, an outcast himself, was the leader of one such group. Or he could accept a duel to the death with knives. In Apache law the next of kin had the right to avenge a murdered relative. In this instance the next of kin was Espejo's elder brother, Garanon.

Jayan stared at the short, muscular young brave he would have to fight if he chose the duel. Garanon's eyes were those of a killer dog waiting only to be let off the leash. Jayan was silent for a few seconds. Then he shrugged his shoulders. "Let it be the knives."

Jayan was taller than Garanon and had a much longer reach. His name, the strong one, had been well earned. But his opponent had the advantage of youth. It was not so much a duel of knives; but of strength and experience against agility and stamina.

The braves quickly formed a circle, about ten paces across, around the two duellists. Neither would be allowed through that circle of men until one or the other was dead.

With an insane ferocity Jayan hurled himself, razor-sharp knife in hand, at the younger man. Garanon glided swiftly away, but not swiftly enough. Blood spurted from a jagged gash in his right arm. Drawing his knife as deftly from his belt with his left hand as he would have with his right, now hanging uselessly, Garanon circled his opponent as warily and smoothly as a jaguar stalking its prey. Gradually he decreased the distance between himself and the older man.

First Garanon lunged forward and Jayan dodged quickly aside. Then Jayan jabbed viciously with his blade and Garanon moved nimbly away. This pattern continued for several minutes.

The blood continued to flow from the wicked slash in the young warrior's right arm. His knees were bent in a forward crouch, the dancing blade in his left hand searching for an opening. But he appeared to be weakening and no longer as mobile. Jayan saw this and made his move. Leaping rapidly to the left, he thrust the point of his weapon towards Garanon's defenceless right side.

Garanon must have been gambling on such a move for he completely out-foxed the more experienced man. His apparent weakness had been a feint. With almost unbelievable speed he transferred the knife to his suddenly rejuvenated right hand and plunged it into Jayan's stomach. The older man's forward rush caused the knife to sink to its hilt. The braves murmured appreciation of Garanon's ruse, but Jayan heard them not.

# CHAPTER TWENTY-TWO

We were moving southwards again, the strain of the raid showing clearly on many faces. It was now the fifteenth day and we were crossing the deadly Jornada del Muerto, the journey of death; more than one hundred miles of waterless desert and choking grey dust. Dust which burned our throats and left our eyes red-rimmed and stinging. Coletto Negro had chosen this route in an attempt to shake off the army which was beginning to close in on all sides.

Only two days before we had run into a small patrol of buffalo soldiers, Negro cavalry, so called because their short, wiry, tightly curled, black hair resembled that on a buffalo's hump. We had killed all ten of them, and their white officer, but two of our own warriors had also fallen.

We had now travelled more than eight hundred miles, killed about sixty of the enemy and captured a herd of perhaps five hundred horses. Our own dead numbered only five, including Jayan. But our luck could not last forever and Coletto Negro had decided it was time to return to Mexico. The border was less than one hundred and fifty miles away. No real distance for an Apache in normal circumstances. But in hostile territory, with the enemy trying to crunch you between its slow-moving, yet powerful, pincer-like jaws, it seemed endless. Scouts were now riding ahead, to the rear and on both flanks to keep us informed of any army movements.

The sixteenth day and fewer than one hundred miles separated us from Mexico. We were within sight of the Rio Grande, which flowed west of the route we were following, when signal flashes in pairs came from our right flank. The final flash pointed south. Soldiers were riding along the river's western banks. Their tactics were obvious. The army had two objectives in mind. To prevent us obtaining water and to keep us east of the Rio Grande; so that when we crossed the border it would be into Texas and not Mexico. Other soldiers were probably waiting for us, or moving northwards to intercept us. We were being herded into a corral like so many wild cattle.

Coletto Negro ordered me to ride out to the scouts on our right to determine the strength of the enemy. Lobo was leading this particular party. He answered my questions briefly. "Few pony soldiers at present. Perhaps thirty or forty. But I think they expect more. There is a shallow stretch in the river four or five miles ahead. If our chief sends enough warriors, the best marksmen, to help me keep these white-eyes pinned down, then the rest of you could cross the horses at the point I speak of. We would rejoin you later. Go now. Time is not our friend in this place."

Immediately I told Coletto Negro of Lobo's plan he saw its logic and sent twenty men, all skilled in the use of the rifle, to join his scout leader. One of them was Cabeza. The chief told him: "Tell Lobo to give us sufficient time to call in the other scouting parties before he opens fire. We will not take long."

Cabeza nodded and rode off with the others towards the Rio Grande. Coletto Negro sent riders out to bring in the scouts ahead, behind and on our left flank. They came in quickly. This made a total of twenty-one to drive the horses. We rode fast. I wished I had been with Cabeza but, although a good shot with a rifle, I was not among the elite.

Including himself and the scouts already with him, Lobo had twenty-five men against a possible forty. The odds were fairly even I thought. But whether the ruse would work was another matter.

As we drove the horses hard towards the river crossing, the dust rose even higher and became an immense mobile cloud which threatened to suffocate us all. We rode blindly. Only the outriders, free of the dense dust cloud, were able to see and it was their cries which guided us. Some of the weaker animals stumbled to their knees, then collapsed completely. The long waterless trek across the Jornada del Muerto was beginning to exact its toll.

The horses, blinded, choking, crazy for water, were stampeding now and almost beyond control. The air was filled with the tattoo of their hooves against the earth. Their shrill cries of fear made it difficult to hear the shouts of the men fighting to guide the thoroughly panicked animals.

Horses, with men astride them, passed momentarily — galloping wildly in all directions. Horses, without men astride them, came into blurred focus for a few seconds — and then disappeared as quickly as they had appeared. Dust, men, dust, horses, dust, noise, dust. It was a nightmare. Except that I was awake and it was real.

Coletto Negro was suddenly alongside, a grey phantom. He was breathless, his voice a harsh, raw sound, barely discernible. "River," he gasped. "Do not let ponies stop to drink. Drive across." Then he was gone.

Behind us somewhere rifles were firing. Without warning I found my mount knee-deep in water. The dust was starting to clear. We were crossing the Rio Grande.

All around me wildly screaming warriors were urging the horse herd forward. Whenever an animal stopped, and lowered its head towards the water, a rider came from nowhere and lashed it into movement again. The chief knew that it was fatal to allow a thirst-crazed horse to drink its fill.

Once across the river, the herd was manoeuvred into a milling circle until it quietened down. As soon as the animals were comparatively calm they were taken back to the water in small groups and permitted to drink. But not to capacity. There was still a long distance between us and Mexico. A horse with a full belly cannot move quickly.

The last one watered, they all stood, sides heaving, heads drooping, grazing at the sparse vegetation on the ground around them. The men now flung themselves eagerly at the water. At that moment it tasted better than the sweetest wine.

Moving again. Not as fast as before and more orderly. It was much easier to control the herd. A drink of water to a tired, frightened horse is like a drink of tequilla to a man in a similar condition.

Yells from the scouts riding to our rear. Men on horses galloping towards us from that direction. I gave a shout of joy. They were Apaches and easily recognizable, well in the lead, was the tall, muscular figure of Cabeza. I started counting as they came closer. Fourteen. Where were the others?

Cabeza reined his horse rapidly beside that of Coletto Negro. "Soldiers came from all sides." His voice was toneless. "We killed and killed. But they were too many. Eleven of our people are dead." He hesitated as the chief glanced backwards at the other survivors riding in. Lobo was not among them. "He is dead," said Cabeza quietly.

Coletto Negro's shoulders sagged. I knew how he felt. Lobo had been my friend also. But it was much worse for my father. To him Lobo had been far more than a friend. He had been a leader in his own right, a counsellor and completely loyal to his chief. No, I did not know how my father felt. My greatest friend, Cabeza, was alive.

With the news that the soldiers were closing in, the drive once more became a headlong flight for the border. Controlling the horses, however, was an easier task than before. Not only were they no longer thirsting for water, but we now had an additional fourteen men helping us. Thirty-five warriors left of the fifty-one who had started out. Sixteen dead. It was a high price to pay for vengeance and a herd of horses. And I knew inside it would be even more costly before we reached Mexico.

Perhaps we will all be killed, I thought. It was difficult to rid my mind of such depressing reflections. Our trail was wide and easy to follow. With its vastly superior numbers, and excellent systems of communication, I felt certain the army would ensnare us before long.

Then it happened. A miracle. The bright blue sky suddenly turned dark grey and we were caught in the midst of a desert storm. Such storms are rare; but when they come they are as no other on earth.

It was like a weird, discordant symphony. The shrill whistle of the wind, the staccato whipcracks of lightning, followed by the powerful rumbling bass of the thunder, and the swish of the torrential rain. Crescendo, diminuendo, crescendo, diminuendo. The symphony varied in intensity according to the whims of nature's orchestra.

Discordant perhaps. But music to our ears. The noise made speech impossible but here and there, through the sheets of rain, I could see faces smiling again.

Knowing that the storm would erase our tracks and make trailing us a perplexing job for the army scouts, the chief decided to make it even harder for them by altering his original straight run for the border. He now veered slightly to the west.

After an hour or so the storm ended as swiftly as it had started. Although of short duration, it had proved an invaluable ally. Previously dry watercourses were once again fast flowing streams. The dust was now a sticky mud in which the ponies sank to their hocks. Difficult going. But even more so for the white-eye soldiers encumbered with the great amount of equipment they always carried into the field.

The sun, once more supreme ruler of the skies after its brief dethronement, caused dense stream to rise from the ground around us. Perspiration flowed freely. The flying insects which invariably follow a storm began to feast on men and horses. It was uncomfortable travelling at best. Yet the warriors, downcast less than two hours before, were smiling. What were these minor irritations compared to the major one we had left behind?

That night we camped within thirty miles of the Mexican border. Feeling safety within their reach the men, among the weariest on earth at the moment, slumped to the ground and slept without first eating. Even those posted as night guards must have been overcome with fatigue, for their senses were not as acute as they should have been. And we paid the price.

Sunrise brought with it a host of blue-clad figures on horseback. They were still about two miles off when they were first spotted, so Coletto Negro decided to make a run for it. We were hungry. But, refreshed by sleep, we drew steadily away from our pursuers who were obviously suffering from their night without rest.

As the sun approached its zenith in the cloudless sky, so our spirits rose with it. Mexico was but a few miles ahead. Seventeen days on a warpath which had taken us across almost a thousand miles of enemy territory.

I turned to Cabeza who was riding furiously beside me. "The country of my birth is never again going to look as beautiful as it will the moment we cross into it," I gasped.

"Although I was born an American I must confess that I have no desire to remain here at this time," he answered breathlessly. "Therefore I must agree with . . ."

His words were interrupted by the sound of trumpet. Galloping swiftly towards us on both flanks were very many pony soldiers. Too many to even estimate their numbers. Our hearts sank. We had escaped those chasing us. But not before they had manoeuvred us cunningly into the jaws of the trap now springing in upon us.

There was no alternative but to run the gauntlet. The horse herd was ahead of us running in a straight line. Rifles began firing on both sides. Bullets whip-cracked viciously through the air around us. One, two, three, four, five warriors tumbled from their mounts but none of us stopped. I lost count of those I saw fall. It was every man for himself. No attempt was made to return the fire. Any delay would have been fatal.

At last we were across the border. The pursuing troopers fired a number of desultory shots in our direction but reined their mounts to a halt. They would not cross into Mexico.

I slowed my pony to a jogtrot. Cabeza reined his horse alongside. His face was strained. He opened his mouth as if to speak but fell against me. There was a large red hole in his back. His mount was covered in its rider's blood.

Leaping from my pony, I lowered him gently from his. My friend, Cabeza, was dying and there was nothing I could do about it. Panic was taking hold of me. I felt like screaming. Screaming at the whole world and the stupidity of man's eternal conflict with his own kind. Conflict that was taking my dearest friend.

"Cuchillo." Cabeza's voice was but a whisper. Blood was now coming from his mouth as well. I knelt beside him as he lay motionless on the ground. There were tears in my eyes and I could not hold them back.

"Do not speak," I told him gently. "Save your strength." It was useless advice, however, for the earth beneath his back was showing dark red stains spreading gradually outwards. He had lost too much blood.

Cabeza raised his head slowly with one final great effort. He had been born a white man but his last words were in Apache. "Sisquism . . . sisquism . . ." "My brother . . . my brother . . ." His head fell back.

For several minutes I knelt beside him sobbing quietly. Perhaps it was longer. I lost track of time.

When I eventually looked up again, it was to see Coletto Negro standing in front of me. "It has been a bad day for the Apache." His words seemed to come from another world. As if only his body remained alive; abandoned by its spirit which was now in some other place.

"And there will be many more such days to come," he continued monotonously, like a robot speaking mechanically. His eyes had lost all lustre. "This raid has cost us forty-two of our finest warriors. We are now but nine. I go to find my people. What will you do?"

"What do you mean?"

"You were born a Mexican," he replied. "Therefore you have a choice. For us there is none."

Some time passed before either of us spoke again.

"What would you do in my place, father?" I asked.

His shoulders straightened somewhat at the word "father" and I felt strangely pleased. "I would take my share of the horses and become a Mexican again," he replied simply. "Start a new life. Your share of the herd would be more than fifty ponies. That would buy a very good new life. But only for a Mexican."

"That is what you would do if you were in my place?"

"Yes, my son, that is what I would do."

I nodded. He was right. The life and people I had loved so much were gone. Yes, he was right. I clasped his hands firmly in mine. Neither of us spoke. I thought I saw tears in his eyes for the first time.

# CHAPTER TWENTY-THREE

With my hair cut short, I reverted to Mexican attire and the Spanish tongue. Posing as a horse-trader, I had no difficulty in selling my share of the stolen herd to the generals of the federal militia, who asked no questions concerning the American brands. Within a short time I had purchased a small hacienda, well-stocked with sheep, and developed into a man of wealth, standing and education. I even remarried. Maria? No, she was my wife's personal servant. She came here with me more than ten years ago, soon after my wife died.

Why here? Well, we had no children and I was alone. Apart from my memories of course. And they are what brought me to this village. An old man has no need of great wealth so I sold the hacienda; keeping sufficient money only to buy this small house and support me while I am of this earth. The rest I gave to the poor. Remember, I was born one of them. And they supplied the Apaches, albeit unwillingly, with life's necessities throughout the many years I lived among those Indians.

Ah, but I ramble on senor. Please come outside and I will show you the two reasons why I chose this place in which to live out my remaining years.

You see those distant mountains to the west? No, they are not the Sierra Madres. But they are so similar in appearance that they remind me of my happiest years. Of Sagozhuni, in particular, and our son. Of Coletto Negro, Cabeza, Lobo and all the other who were my friends for so long. In retrospect, I can see that to the civilization which then existed, they appeared as a bunch of cruel, ragged, filthy, evil-smelling savages. But to me, although I came to hate their cruelty, they represented things entirely different. Independence, kindness to their own and, above all, pride in their manhood. They made me a man. That is one reason I choose to live here.

The second is that this is the village in which I was born. You see that spot over there . . . No, not there. But to the right of where your automobile is parked. Yes, just there. That is where my parents were killed and I was taken by the Apaches. I rode across many thousands of miles for almost twenty years before I again saw this place. It was a long ride home.